VIRUS ON ORBIS 1

PJ HAARSMA

This is a work of fiction. Names, characters, places, and incidents are either products of the author's imagination or, if real, are used fictitiously.

Copyright © 2021 by PJ Haarsma

All rights reserved. No part of this book may be reproduced, transmitted, or stored in an information retrieval system in any form or by any means, graphic, electronic, or mechanical, including photocopying, taping, and recording, without prior written permission from the publisher.

Second Paperback edition 2021

ISBN: 978-1-953505-03-3

The Library of Congress has cataloged the hardcover edition as follows:

Haarsma, PJ.
The softwire: virus on Orbis 1 / PJ Haarsma. — 2nd ed.
p. cm.

Summary:
[1. Computers — Fiction. 2. Orphans — Fiction. 3. Science fiction.]
I. Title. II. Title: Virus on Orbis One.
PZ7.H111325So 2006
[Fic] — dc22 2006046285

For Marisa

Foreword

by Nathan Fillion

Science fiction means a lot to me.

It always has.

The questions, "What comes next?", and "How will we change as technology advances?" have constantly inspired me. The imagining of where we are going becomes a comment on where we are now. It all becomes so much more real for me when sci-fi accurately predicts a technology or social norm. I can't remember who was it that said in the future, everyone would have their own tv show, but they nailed it. Star Trek introduced us to the communicator, and we've already left flip phone technology so far behind us.

PJ creates an entire universe in the Rings of Orbis series, so far removed from the universe we know, but leaves our humanity intact enough that it's still familiar. The intricacies of differing cultures, politics, and economy all play into one young man's journey. If you are looking for something entirely new to sink your sci-fi teeth into, I know you'll enjoy Rings of Orbis Series.

"I can see them! I can see the Rings of Orbis!" Theodore Malone cried, and a stampede of kids charged toward the observation deck.

"I bet you're dying to see Orbis, aren't you, malf?" Randall Switzer said, digging his foot a little deeper into my face. In fact, I was. I'd waited twelve years to see my new home, wishing every day was this day. But I wouldn't dare let him know that.

"I can kill a little more time down here," I said from the floor.

Switzer snickered and shifted more weight onto his foot. I hate feet. Feet with shoes, feet with socks, but worst of all — like the sweaty one grinding into my cheek — I hate bare feet.

"What are you doing, Switzer?" Maxine Bennett said.

"Why do you care?" he replied.

"I figure you've got another microsecond before Mother knows what you're doing. I do not want to be near all this food when it turns the gravity off," Max warned him.

You don't want to be on a toilet, either, I thought, but I didn't feel this was the right time to bring that up.

"Why doesn't he just *tell* Mother to rescue him?" Switzer said.

And there it was, the thing that separated me

from everyone else on the seed-ship. While the others communicated with Mother through their O-dat displays or heard Mother over the cent-com, I was the only one who actually *spoke* with it. *It,* not *her* — Mother was the ship's computer that had saved and cared for all of us after the adults died and that had guided the *Renaissance* to its destination — the Rings of Orbis.

The thing was, not everyone believed me, especially Switzer. Our self-proclaimed leader took great pleasure in discrediting my ability and making me the laughingstock of nearly everyone else on the seed-ship. But things were about to change. The ride was almost over — thank the universe.

"So now you believe him when he says he can talk to the computer?" Max said.

"I just asked him what his hurry was," Switzer said, beginning to sound bored. "He knows the rules."

"Answer him, JT," she said.

Actually, I had come into the contest tank looking for Max. I needed her help getting something out of the computer. Something Mother wouldn't let me have, but I didn't want Switzer to know about it. Silently, I stared at her feet (at least *she* wore shoes).

"Stubborn doesn't work," Switzer reminded me.

Finally, I lied and told him, "I was just looking for my sister."

"Baby-malf? Why would I care about her?" he said, raking his toes one more time across my nose as he released me. "See how easy that was? Come on, Max, let's see if that freak really did spot the rings."

I sat up and watched them leave. My quest would have to wait.

I found Ketheria standing alone in the eighty-meter glass tube that connected the common galleries and the contest tank. My sister, who was five years younger than me, was fiercely independent. Then again, so were all the children on the *Renaissance*. Thirteen years with the supervision of only a computer can do that. Together, Ketheria and I squeezed to the front of the crowd and squished our faces against the glass as the giant seed-ship came about.

There they were: the Rings of Orbis — four colossal planet-like rings floating around an invisible wormhole. *What will it be like there?* I wondered for the trillionth time. *What will happen now — to us?* I had been waiting my whole life for this moment. After 253 years in space (we spent most of the trip as nothing more than a few cells frozen in plastic dishes), the *Renaissance* would finally set down on the ground, or the ring, that is.

I tapped on the glass for magnification, and the four massive rings filled the void in front of us. For a split second I wondered how my parents would have felt if they had been alive to see this day.

I squeezed Ketheria's hand and said, "Look, between the rings, those are the moons." I pointed. "See? Ki and Ta."

Ketheria didn't say anything to me. It wasn't that she didn't know what they were. She just never said anything to anyone. She was almost eight years old and had never spoken a single word. I looked out for her because she was the only family I had and we were the only siblings on the *Renaissance*. I kind of liked that.

"I can't wait to get off this ship," I whispered to her. "Finally, a place we can call home."

Ketheria looked up at me. She smiled and squeezed my hand again. It was reassuring because I really had no idea what Orbis would be like. There would be a whole new set of rules, but I felt confident that any alien rules had to be better than Switzer's.

I stared at my new home. Our parents had signed a contract to work on Orbis for four years — one year on each ring. In return, their Guarantors, administrators for the Trading Council, paid for their travel and would sponsor their citizenship on Orbis when their work was done. But the untimely death of all our parents meant that Ketheria and I, along with every other kid on the *Renaissance,* were now at the mercy of the Citizens of Orbis.

"Are you bleeding this time?" Max asked me, popping up on my left.

"No," I said.

She kept her eyes focused on Orbis and let out a

deep breath. "I can't wait to see what makes those rings tick," she said.

I like Max. She never makes fun of me about Mother, like most of the other kids. And she's better than anyone when it comes to taking things apart and putting them back together, although they usually wind up performing an entirely different function when she's done.

"Well, I'm going to finish packing," she said.

As she turned to leave, I scanned the tube for Switzer. He was at the other end, preaching to his bootlickers.

"Max?" I called, and she looked back over her shoulder. "I need your help with something."

She pointed at herself and said, "Me?"

I nodded.

"Sure," she said.

"Sit here," I told Max, pointing to the O-dat display in my room. It was actually my parents' quarters. Most of the little ones still stayed in the nurture pods, while the older kids had scooped up the private rooms.

She read my screen. "Restricted? I didn't know any files on the *Renaissance* were restricted."

"Neither did I."

"Mother, please access all research files, personal notes, and log entries from my parents," I said out loud.

"Yes, Johnny," Mother said. The reply filtered into my mind in Mother's voice: the effort to sound human was a little overdone.

"Is Mother talking to you right now?" Max asked.

"Yes. Mother, can you respond using the centcom? This room only, please."

"Certainly," it said. "But the reconstructed quantized waveform created inside Max's auditory canals would only sound like static to her."

"Oh, thanks," I told the computer.

"No need to thank me, Johnny. As you've reminded me many times, I'm just a computer with no feelings."

I smiled.

"Can Mother do that? Why don't you get the computer to respond out loud all the time? Then maybe Switzer won't bother you so much."

I shook my head. "I wish. Watch the screen," I told her. "Mother, would you access all files that make reference to my parents, please?"

"I've already performed that task," the computer replied.

"I know," I said. "But I need the restricted files, too."

"Why would anything on the ship be restricted?" Max asked.

"Wait," I whispered to her.

"Mother, under which category are the restricted files located?" I said.

"Research," the computer replied.

Of course, I'd already asked Mother all these questions. I was just repeating it all for Max. "Why did you never tell me about these files before?"

"You never asked for the restricted files before this cycle," the computer said.

Max looked at the screen. "Ask it why I can't see them on the terminal."

"Why can't I see them on the terminal, Mother?"

"They are restricted."

I threw my arms up in the air. "'Restricted,' it keeps telling me. And there's *three hundred and twelve* of them!"

What made it so frustrating was that I thought I had read everything about my parents. It's what I did. Despite the thousands of hours of entertainment files and the games Mother programmed in the contest tank, I often spent my free time searching the computer, reading everything my parents had left there: all their letters, their diaries, their research; all their hopes for the future. I read about my mother's fears after the cryogenic sleepers failed and the ship lost thirty crew members. She worried that she and my dad would die in the sleepers before my sister and I were born. My mother was right. The cryogenic sleepers did fail again, and the entire crew was lost. The only survivors were the embryos — us.

"I want those files," I told Max.

"Why me? Why didn't you get one of your friends to help?"

She was being polite. She knew I had only one friend on the *Renaissance,* and Theodore was too shy to do anything as *irregular* as this.

"If you can't get at them, I figure no one else can," I told her.

Max smiled. "You're definitely right about that," she said. "Now stand back and let me see why this computer is being so stubborn."

Max pulled a thin folded piece of material out of her pocket. She slapped it on the wall next to my display and tried to smooth out the wrinkles.

"Where did you get that?"

"I made it."

"You made it?"

"Well, actually, I took apart one of the O-dat displays. I only wanted the organic polymer, anyway," she said.

"What's it for?"

"Mother's always destroying any little patch or workaround I make. This keeps them private."

"Oh. Will that help?"

"It should," she said, and pulled her brown hair into a ponytail before attacking the display. Whenever I watched her on the *Renaissance,* Max was always trying to be one of the boys, but it isn't hard to tell Max is a girl: she's very pretty. I'd never let her hear me say it, though.

I watched her work on the display. Everyone liked Max. She never stuck with one group of kids. Instead she liked to get involved in everyone's business. Not like me. Besides Theodore and Ketheria, I wasn't much for groups.

"What are you doing?" Mother asked.

"I need those restricted files," I answered.

"I'm sorry, Johnny. If you continue, I will shut down this terminal," Mother warned.

"Keep going," I whispered to Max.

"Johnny?" Mother said.

"Fine, Mother, we'll stop."

But I motioned to Max to keep going. "Hurry," I whispered.

Max was typing frantically into the terminal when the power went off.

"Darn," I said. But Max flashed a devilish grin. She removed a small gold disc from the terminal.

"Can Mother hear me?"

"No," I said.

"Good. I couldn't crack it, but I did create a hyperlink on a memory disc. The files are not actually copied, but I can find them quickly from a remote location," Max said. "I made a mirror image on this disc that links back to your parents' restricted files. As long as the *Renaissance* stays parked on Orbis 1, we should have fun hacking in from any terminal on Orbis." Max stood there smiling, with her hands on her hips.

"What if there are no computers on Orbis?"

Max frowned. "Of course, there are."

I cradled the disc in my fingers. This was the only thing on the ship that was of any importance to me. The rest I could leave: the *Renaissance* was not my home anymore.

"That's it, then," I said. "I'm all packed."

2

During our study sessions on the *Renaissance,* Mother made sure we knew everything we could about what was going to be our new home. We knew that Orbis is a system of four rings: Orbis 1, 2, 3, and 4. Our destination was Orbis 1.

I knew that each ring is 9,848 kilometers in circumference and 32.82 kilometers wide. These rings maintain their position around the massive wormhole by floating at the natural Lagrange points created by the moons, Ki and Ta. I pictured them as giant Ferris wheels, just like the ones I'd seen in the history archives from Earth. Only these are much bigger and float in space.

We also learned what little was known about the alien civilization that first discovered the wormhole. This fold in space brought the Ancients, as they are now called, from their galaxy to the moons of Orbis ninety thousand years ago. The Ancients built the rings to stabilize the wormhole and harvest the lucrative energy crystals discovered deep within the moons. Ki and Ta were the only things left behind after the wormhole formed and swallowed up everything in its path.

But no one owns the rings. The alien race that created them mysteriously disappeared more than sixty thousand years ago. Mother attempted to teach us about their understanding of the universe in our studies — odd stuff about cosmic energy and nodes — but most of it I never understood. The Ancients also believed that any choice we made affected the entire universe. Somehow I doubted that whatever I did could affect someone on Orbis, much less in another galaxy somewhere.

The four rings, the wormhole, and the two moons are now governed by a race of alien philosophers known as the Keepers. The Keepers worship the Ancients, but the teachings of the Ancients are actually protected by incomprehensible creatures called Nagools. They were even more confusing to me, and I usually fell asleep during that part of my studies.

The Keepers now monitor all travel through the wormhole and create the rules of Orbisian society. Only they can grant someone citizenship on the rings. The Trading Council, elected by the First Families after the War of Ten Thousand Rotations and approved by the Keepers, controls the economy on the rings. They must also provide for the Keepers. In return, the Keepers do not seek economic power or exert control over the Citizens' business dealings. Their only concern is to maintain the well-being of Orbis and to protect the sanctity of the rings in hope that the Ancients may one day return. They're still waiting.

Once the Rings of Orbis came into view, normal activity on the seed-ship stopped. Mother tried to get us to continue with our studies, but the atmosphere was that of Birth Day, and everyone just did what they wanted. Most of the children sat in the observation tube staring at the rings, while others played games like Ring Defender or Diggum in the contest tank.

I watched as Ketheria played Quest Nest with her friends. In Quest Nest, partners searched for each other in a multidimensional maze, or nest, as we called it. Once they found each other, the pair had to get out through the maze, but the maze would always change. Mother would also throw in a few surprises from the interactive 4-D walls. The first pair out won.

This game Mother almost caught Ketheria with a crazed frontier pilot, but Ketheria hit him squarely in the head with an immobility cube. I always preferred dropping Mother's little surprises with the alien plasma gun, but not Ketheria. She emerged from the maze victorious.

"Way to go, Ketheria!" I shouted as Theodore came and sat next to me.

"JT, I've been looking everywhere for you," he said.

Theodore was the same age as me. Actually, half the kids on the ship were the same age as me. After the adults died, the computer's emergency program decided when the time was right for the embryos to be born. Half the children on the ship shared one Birth Day, and the other half, including my sister, all shared another.

"What's wrong?" I said.

"Didn't you see the message? On the O-dats?"

"A message?" Mother would have mentioned a message to me. "What does it say?" I got up and went straight to the first display I could find.

"Same message, one thousand two hundred and twelve times."

"You checked every display?"

Theodore shrugged. He likes to count things. Why? I don't know. He doesn't talk with too many people, so I figure he does it to keep himself busy and away from —

Switzer shoved me aside and grabbed the display. "Get away from that," he barked at us, and read the screen. "Delivery? What do they mean, 'delivery'?"

His best friend, Dalton, stood guard, scowling at us while Switzer pored over the message. Dalton was a digital copy of Switzer, only not as sharp.

"It says they're sending someone to greet us and prepare us for our *delivery*," Switzer said. "I don't like the sound of that." He spun the display away and elbowed past me. "Get out of the way, split-screen."

Theodore watched as they left the tank. "It took him thirty-six words before he insulted us. He's getting slow."

But I didn't care. Someone from Orbis had finally contacted us. This was exciting. I turned the screen back toward myself and read the entire message:

welcome
we gratefully await your arrival
a keeper has been sent to greet you and prepare you for delivery
please anticipate this arrival in two cycles
welcome
keepers of orbis

"Delivery?" I said. "That is an odd choice of words."

"We're lucky they know our language," Theodore said.

"It's awesome, isn't it? You don't know how many questions I have. I can't wait to get some answers."

Theodore pointed at the screen. "It says we're to be ready in two cycles."

A cycle is like a day on Earth, only a few hours shorter. "Four diams make a spoke; four spokes make a cycle; four cycles make a phase; four phases make a set; ten sets make a rotation." Theodore and I recited the Orbisian year in unison: something Mother had drilled into our brains since birth.

When the cycle finally arrived, I was pressed against the glass of the observation tube. The *Renaissance* dwarfed the tiny craft of the alien who was coming to welcome us to Orbis. Our seed-ship was large enough to hold forty-five hundred people for up to three hundred years. Except now it barreled through space with a passenger list of only two hundred children, and every last one of us was in the tube.

I was so excited, I couldn't even breathe. The alien's vessel silently docked with ours, and we scrambled to the docking bay. I ducked under Switzer's arm and raced down the maze of corridors. I needed to be there first. My skin prickled from the cool air of the portal, and I swallowed hard, finally allowing myself to breathe. I wanted to know everything about my new home — all the great things about the Rings of Orbis.

Then, for the first time in 253 years, the seal on the entry door hissed open. Rancid-smelling steam stung my nostrils, and I covered my nose. Over my hand I could see a slender, hooded creature dressed in a soft purple robe moving toward us. He ducked to pass through the entry — the alien must have been close to three meters tall — then pulled his hood back to reveal his translucent blue complexion. His eyes were like marbles without eyelids — all four of them.

The alien had two heads.

"Hello, I am the Keeper known as Theylor," said the alien's left head as he bowed slightly but never stopped looking at us.

"I have attempted to learn your Earth language to assist in your delivery," Theylor's right head said. "That way we can understand one another until you receive your implants and the translation codec," Theylor's left head continued, finishing the thought.

Theodore, who was next to me by now, whispered, "Implants? Translation codec? What's he talking about?"

I didn't respond. I just shook my head and stared at the alien. This was the first time I'd ever seen a being other than a human. It took a moment to sink in. Each of Theylor's heads was long and bald, and his skin looked as thin as a silicon wafer. I looked around. I wasn't the only one staring. We were all gaping at the Keeper. Finally, one of the younger kids spoke.

"Why do you have two heads?" she asked the alien.

"Why do you have only one?" both heads replied, smiling.

"I only need one."

"Well, I need two. That way I can see everything that is going on around me. My work on Orbis is very important, you know."

Theylor's two heads might take some getting used to.

"I am here to answer any questions you may have and prepare the seed-ship for docking," he continued.

The shock of the Keeper's appearance was immediately replaced with the desire to know more about Orbis. I wasn't the only one with questions. The docking bay erupted in a chorus of voices.

"Please, children, one at a time," Theylor pleaded. "Maybe we can move to a more comfortable area?"

"We can go to the rec room," I offered.

Theylor looked at me for what seemed to be an

unusually long time. I looked at Theodore. He was looking at Theylor looking at me. So was Switzer. I didn't like that. Theylor's gaze was cold, as though he wasn't just *looking* at me but seeing right inside me. I rubbed the back of my neck as the alien stared. *Why is he singling me out?* I thought. Maybe he didn't understand what I said.

"I'll show you," Switzer interrupted, but Theylor never stopped looking at me.

"Lead the way, please," he finally said, and Switzer elbowed his way past me.

That was fine with me. *Let Switzer take the lead,* I thought, and I slipped back into the crowd. In the rec room we all surrounded the Keeper, but I hung back. Suddenly, I didn't have very many questions to ask the Keeper.

"What will my room be like on Orbis?" Switzer asked.

"Room? Things are different on Orbis, different from how they have been on your seed-ship. We have tried our best to imitate the life you are used to until you assimilate to life on Orbis."

"Are there other children?" Max asked.

"The Citizens have children. Some species, however, have different cultures and different manners in which they handle their offspring. You will discover all of them during your stay on Orbis 1."

"What does the food taste like?" someone asked.

"Wonderful. We have food from every corner of

the universe, especially in the markets, where you can barter for superb items from anywhere," said Theylor's left head.

This is going to be great, I said to myself. I looked at Ketheria and smiled. I knew how much she loved food.

We were all talking to each other. The chatter grew louder, but Theylor kept answering questions. Then the Keeper asked a question.

"May I meet with the adults now?" he said.

Everyone fell silent. Adults? *He doesn't know.*

"They're dead," one kid said.

Both of Theylor's heads said, "Dead? All of them?"

"Before we were born," Switzer said.

"This is not as we expected," he said.

Theylor's heads moved slightly from side to side, almost as if he were having a conversation with himself, but no words were spoken aloud. Finally, Max stood up.

"Hello, my name is Maxine Bennett," she said, interrupting the Keeper's thoughts.

"Hello, Maxine," Theylor replied.

"You can call me Max. Everyone does."

"All right, Max. Do you have a question?" Theylor asked.

"Yes, I do. Who will look after us?" Max asked.

"We don't need anyone to look after us," Switzer said defiantly.

Theylor looked at Switzer. "Well, your Guarantor will now," he said after a long pause.

"We will have to designate you several Guarantors, I suppose. This was already established for the adults. You will live with your Guarantor and work for your Guarantor."

"Work?" Dalton said.

Things suddenly got very quiet. None of us were very fond of chores. This was obvious from the mess we'd left on the ship — but *work*? That was a whole new concept.

"Why, yes. Your parents were sponsored by a group of investors who paid for their travel in exchange for four years of work on Orbis — one year on each ring. Since the adults from the *Renaissance* are all dead, the Council for the Center for Impartial Judgment and Fair Dealing will have to grant the investors ownership to replace that debt."

"Ownership? Ownership of what?" I asked.

"Ownership of you, of all of you," Theylor answered, and gestured with his hand. His thin red fingernails clicked against the dark metal bobbles that trimmed his velvet robe. It was the only sound in the room.

Can this be true? I wondered. *Ketheria and I are now the property of some alien?*

"What does that mean?" I asked the two-headed alien.

"You will work for your Guarantors in exchange for your existence on Orbis. Your parents' debt must be repaid," Theylor said matter-of-factly.

"But only four rotations. That's all, right?" I said

to Theylor.

"After four rotations, the trading council will review your work record. Only then will they decide if their debt has been repaid."

"You mean we could have to work longer," I said.

"It is possible. It will depend upon your behavior during your work rule."

"Could we end up working on Orbis forever?" Max asked.

"That has happened only on rare occasions," the Keeper replied.

Forever? Forever! The thought screamed inside my head. Why would my parents do this?

"And what if I don't want to?" Switzer asked.

"I do not understand," Theylor said.

"What if I refuse? What if I don't want to be a slave for some alien?" Switzer continued.

I could see by the puzzled look on the Keeper's face — both of his faces — that he did not understand our reluctance to accept this arrangement.

"Do you mean you would refuse the honor of fulfilling your parents' debt, let alone the opportunity to live on Orbis?" Theylor asked.

"Absolutely," Switzer said.

"You are now the property of the Guarantors. That will be up to them," Theylor said.

"Has anyone ever refused this — this *honor*?" I asked.

"Actually, yes. I do recall some examples."

"What happened?" Max asked.

"They were extinguished," Theylor said.

"You mean killed?" I said.

"Yes. I mean killed."

"Every time?" Switzer said.

"Every time."

Some of the children left the rec room after Theylor's pronouncement. I just sat there, too stunned to say anything. *Slaves?* When no more questions were asked, Theylor broke the silence.

"I am surprised this information has disturbed you. Trust me when I tell you that this is a very wise decision for your care and welfare at this time. Once your debt is repaid, you, too, will be allowed to apply for Citizen status or have the choice to take a journey through the wormhole. You may choose anywhere in the universe as your destination, but I am sure most of you will decide to stay."

This did not cheer me up. For so long I had dreamed about my life on Orbis. But now my freedom would be gone the second I stepped off the ship. I didn't know what to think.

"I will leave you now. I will be back in one cycle to collect all of you and your belongings," Theylor said, and he left the ship.

I sat in the tube and stared at the rings. *Why?* I wondered. Why did they do it? Why did our parents want to come here? Did they know *we* would be put to work? I looked to the rings for answers but found only more questions.

The atmosphere on the *Renaissance* was very different now while we waited to dock on Orbis 1. I didn't think the younger children really understood what was happening, but I worried they might. I went to see what Ketheria was doing.

I found her in my room, rummaging through the items I planned to leave behind. Clutched in her right hand was a plastic bag, and she was stuffing shirts, shoes, and even toilet paper inside. Pretty much everything she saw.

"You can't take all that stuff," I said. "Besides, that's mine." I pulled the shirt from her bag.

I sat on my sleeper and looked up at my sister.

"Ketheria," I said, "do you understand what's happening? This isn't what I expected."

She looked away and continued to pillage my room. She soon discovered the memory disc Max had made for me. "Don't touch that," I said. "I am taking that with me." She put it back next to the O-dat. "C'mon, Ketheria. Does this feel right to you?"

Ketheria set the bag in the center of my room, then rifled her way to the bottom. She pulled something out and placed it in my hand.

"What's this?"

It was a crude piece of jewelry cut from the organic polymer of an O-dat display, like the stuff Max carried in her pocket. A small chip was forcibly melted to the back of it, and the whole thing hung on a piece of wire, six-gauge, I think.

"Did you make this?" I said, but Ketheria shook her head.

"Did Max make it?"

She nodded and squeezed the strange trinket. The faces of our parents alternated on the mini O-dat. They were the same rank-and-file pictures that were stored on the ship's computer. I stared at the face of my mother. I could see Ketheria's fine cheekbones. She also has Mom's shiny auburn hair. We both do. Mom's eyes, too, not brown but almost yellow. Dad's picture was different, though. I couldn't find Ketheria in his face. His was too rugged and leathery. He was a man's man. I hoped to look like him one day.

"I can't take this," I said, and handed it back to her.

She pushed my hand away.

"No, Ketheria, this is yours. This is special." I returned it to her bag.

Ketheria took the piece of jewelry, put it in my hand, and pushed it against my chest.

"What?" I didn't understand. "This is yours."

She pushed again. I felt the wire pressing through my shirt.

"All right, I'll take it." I held it up. "Thank you," I told her, and she smiled.

I put the piece in my pocket along with the memory disc and grabbed her bag. "C'mon, I'll help you," I said. "We're docking soon. Let's see what our new life's gonna be like."

Ketheria pointed to another full bag in the corner. I grabbed it, and we headed out the door.

Ketheria and I reached the ship's docking bay just as the *Renaissance* was making its final maneuvers. We stood waiting with all the other children as the *Renaissance* made contact with the Orbis 1 station. Ketheria grabbed my hand. I knew she was nervous. I was, too. But I was also excited. The inside of the seed-ship was my whole universe, and now I was about to leave behind everything I knew and enter a completely new world. What would it smell like, look like, feel like? Who would I meet there?

The ship jostled as it made contact with Orbis. *We're here,* I thought. Then, without warning, the *Renaissance* twisted from a massive shock wave and I was thrown across the room. Everything slowed down: I saw my sister's bag burst open and soar across the docking bay. Somewhere, maybe next to me, I heard Theodore yell.

"What's happening?"

Max screamed. The seal on the door ripped, and the thick metal portal crumpled like paper under the ship's weight.

"Get away from there!" someone yelled; I think it was me.

An alarm ripped through the bay as the breach gobbled up the oxygen. But that was nothing compared with the horrifying screech that poured in through the tattered opening. The sound vibrated my bones. I covered my ears, but the sound was inescapable. It was inside me, clawing at my every nerve ending.

"We have to get out of here!" Max shouted over the noise, and I grabbed Ketheria. I began pushing people toward the door. "Back into the ship! Everyone, *now*!"

We scrambled. Some appeared hurt — just cuts and bruises. I helped a few more kids to their feet, but my lungs struggled for oxygen and the temperature in the docking bay was plummeting.

"Seal the door, JT!" Max yelled.

My ears were still ringing as the last child escaped the ship's docking bay. I hit the control panel, sealing off the deathly chamber. Then I looked back through the portal and saw all our possessions abandoned on the floor.

"What was that?" Theodore said.

That was not a good start.

After checking that Ketheria was not hurt, the three of us bolted to the observation tube to get a glimpse of the damage.

"What do you think happened?" Theodore asked, rubbing a bump on his head.

"I have no idea. Maybe they had problems docking the ship," I said.

"The ship was already docked," Max said, running past me.

When we reached the observation tube, we all scurried to get a better view. Any damage was blocked from our sight, but it was obvious that the *Renaissance* was not sitting straight in the port. I could see a flurry of activity around the point where the ship had made contact with Orbis I — the point where we had just been waiting. Blue electric light emanated from small robotic welders already hovering over the damage and repairing the docking station.

The three large O-dats on the entrance wall flickered to life with an image of the Keeper Theylor.

"Does anyone need medical attention?" Theylor asked.

"Not that we can see," Theodore said.

"What happened, Theylor?" I asked.

"First indications point to a small foreign codec within the port computer array. It is very unorthodox. Everything should be repaired shortly, and we will have you in your new home in less than a cycle. Until then, please relax, and I will return shortly." Theylor's image disappeared.

"What kind of place is this revolving junk heap?" Switzer spat.

"Shut up, Switzer," Max said, but he was already huddled with his gang. Max turned to me and said quietly, "I've read about the central computer on Orbis, and it does not make mistakes — ever. The thing is practically a sentient being, with more processing power and backup systems than an army of computer scientists. What just happened *should not* have happened."

"You're talking about the computer that controls every aspect of our new home?" I said.

"Yep."

Normally Max did not share these things with

me, but then again this was not normal. I leaned in close to Max and said, "Don't tell the other children what you just told me, okay? You know — about the central computer?"

"Why?" Max asked.

"Please?" I said, and Max shrugged.

"I'm going to see if Mother can tell me anything about what just happened."

"Let me know what you find out," she asked, as if we'd been friends forever.

I nodded. I liked having Max as a friend.

I returned to my room while most of the kids stayed and watched the repairs.

"Mother, can you tell me what happened with the docking procedure?"

There was no response from the computer.

"Mother?"

Still nothing.

"Very odd. Mother, access all correspondence with Orbis."

No answer. Mother was just not there.

It was strange and unsettling not to get a response. I always felt the comfort of that annoying computer just a question away. I attempted to log on to the O-dat to check the damage but still got no response. What could have happened out there in the docking bay?

In the dining hall I examined the chow synth dispensers to see what was available. Not a lot. Anything behind the little plastic doors must have been getting old, anyway. I settled for a hydroponic apple and sat in front of an O-dat. I tried again to call up Mother, but there was nothing. Absolutely nothing. I checked the connections and even attempted a local reboot, but still nothing. The computer on the *Renaissance* was dead.

I moved to another display, but I was stopped by a large group of children entering the dining hall. Randall Switzer was leading them.

"We're taking over the *Renaissance* and getting out of here," Switzer said.

"What?"

"You heard me, Turnbull. We're not sticking around here to be the slaves of some freak-headed alien. None of us traveled halfway across the galaxy for this."

"Does everyone feel this way?" I asked. Then I saw Max step out from behind Switzer. I was stunned.

"Max?"

"Your new little girlfriend here told me about the central computer. Do you really want to get on that ring when the computer that runs the whole place can't dock a ship?"

"You don't know that," I said.

"JT, just listen to what he has to say," Max said.

"Why? I'm just as worried, but this isn't the answer. I mean, c'mon. What did you expect? Our parents made a deal with the Trading Council. Why wouldn't they want us to honor that?"

Ketheria was there, too. At first I thought she was with them, but she pushed through the crowd and stood next to me.

"Why do you need me, Switzer? You haven't said ten words to me in the past thirteen years that weren't some sort of insult," I said.

"JT, we need you to ask Mother to help us," Max said.

"But I just —"

"Are you with us or are you going to be a problem?" Switzer demanded.

He was not going to take no for an answer. He motioned to Dalton, who revealed a metal oxygen cylinder he was hiding behind his back.

"Have you all gone crazy?" I asked.

"Just do it, JT. Ask Mother," Max pleaded.

I slowly shook my head as Dalton smacked the metal cylinder against his hand. For a moment the situation reminded me of those entertainment studies Mother played for us in the contest tank — movies, Mother called them. Someone was always being forced to do something they didn't want to do and to choose between two sides, each as bad as the other. Now the choice was either life on Orbis as a slave or life on an errant seed-ship with Switzer as captain. I really didn't see much difference.

"It doesn't matter, anyway," I said.

"Yes, it does," Switzer said.

"It doesn't matter, because Mother no longer responds."

"JT, please help us," Max said.

"No, I'm serious. The computer will not respond to me anymore."

I looked to Ketheria for an answer. She knew I was telling the truth.

Then Switzer stepped forward and snatched her up. "Maybe you need some more persuasion," he said.

"Switzer, don't!" Theodore shouted.

I saw the panic in Ketheria's eyes. My mind went blank and I went on autopilot. I reached out and grabbed Switzer, wrenching his arm away. Ketheria fell to the side, but Max caught her. Switzer responded quickly, knocking me down with his forearm. Instantly, I spun on the ground and swiped his feet out from under him. Switzer fell to the floor with a thud.

"Stop it!" someone screamed.

But Switzer was bigger than me and quicker. Before I could get to him, he grabbed my arm, twisted it behind my back, then used his extra weight to grind me into the floor. A white-hot bolt of pain shot through my body.

"This is not the time to start being brave, Turnbull. Tell Mother we want to take the *Renaissance* out of here, now," Switzer demanded, and cranked my arm up a notch.

"Stop it, Switzer!" Max said.

"What do you care?" Switzer snapped.

"I'm not following you if you're going to treat us like this," she said.

"How do you think those Keepers are gonna treat us?" Switzer picked me up and slammed me onto the floor again. "Talk to Mother!" he demanded.

There was nothing I could do. "You don't understand. The ship's computer has gone off-line. I think the Keepers now have control of our ship."

"Or maybe I was right all along and you never could talk to Mother," Switzer said, leaning over and breathing in my ear.

"I don't care what you believe, Switzer. I only know what I can and cannot do, and right now I cannot reach Mother. Beat me with that cylinder if you want, but it will not give you control of the ship's computer."

"Get off him," someone else said.

"Switzer, I don't want to be a slave to some alien any more than you do, but don't you think our parents knew what they were doing?" I said.

"You're an idiot, Turnbull. We're nothing more than cargo to those two-headed freaks. C'mon," Switzer said, getting off me and motioning to the crowd.

Max and a couple of kids helped me up. Only Switzer's loyal followers stood by his side. The other kids did not move, including Max.

"Come on!" he said.

"I'm not going with you," Max said.

"Me neither," said another.

"I'll try my luck on Orbis," someone else said.

"Idiots. Then we'll take the ship ourselves," Switzer said, and he and his group pushed through the crowd.

"Do you think it was wise not to get Mother

involved?" Theodore said as we watched them go. "You could have gotten hurt; besides, they don't know how to fly this ship."

"I'm telling the truth, Theodore. Mother no longer has control of the *Renaissance*. We belong to the Citizens of Orbis now."

3

I sat in my room playing with the piece of jewelry Ketheria had given me. I was now more confused than ever. Switzer's endeavor to take over the seed-ship amounted to nothing more than banging on the control-room doors. The Keepers had locked us out. But that didn't prevent Switzer and his gang from running through the ship pounding on everything they could find.

Did he have a point? I stared at the face of my father on the tiny display. *Why did you come here? What were you going to do?* I looked at my mother's face, but I didn't see an answer there, either.

"What are you doing?" Theodore said, and I jumped.

"You scared me," I said, slipping the picture of my parents into my pocket.

"You thinking about what I'm thinking about?"

"You mean Switzer?"

"Yeah. I'm glad he didn't get through that door."

"I know. Imagine what that would be like." We both laughed.

"I'm still scared, though," he said.

"Me, too. But I can't help but think our parents took this trip for a better life. They must have known something we don't. You know what?" I said. "I'm going to get off this ship and find out what that was. I'm going to do everything I can to make Orbis my new home."

"Well, it's waiting for us."

"The docking bay's fixed?"

Theodore nodded.

"Let's go, then," I said.

When we returned to the restored docking bay, there was no need to help Ketheria with her things. She had none. The repairs to the docking station had destroyed whatever items we had left behind in our scramble to safety. Fortunately, the computer disc Max had made for me remained neatly tucked away in my pocket.

Ketheria fidgeted next to me.

"Don't be afraid," I said to her. "We're doing the right thing. I just know it." But I didn't know why.

The doors hissed open and I braced myself for another glitch in the central computer, but it didn't come.

"Hello, children," Theylor said, entering the docking bay. "Welcome to Orbis 1. Follow me."

This is it, I thought as I stepped into the clear tube that stretched from the ship to the docking port on the ring. Behind me floated the seed-ship and a life I was eager to abandon — in front of me waited the New Arrival Processing Center on Orbis 1.

It was like nothing I could ever have imagined.

My nose filled with a silky sweet smell, laden with alien pollen from flowering plants that cascaded down the towering walls. And the aliens! Hundreds of them scurried about the atrium, basking in a pink glow from gigantic crystals that floated above our heads. All I could do was stare. It was a stark contrast to the interior of our gray, lifeless seed-ship.

"Wow!" Theodore said.

"Wow, wow, and wow," Max repeated.

Sculptures cut from smoky blue crystals bigger than Theylor peered down at us from cavities carved into the sloped stone walls. Melodic notes dampened the clamor of the port. It was sweeter than any music I had ever heard from Earth. If I wanted to describe paradise, this would be it. Instantly, I understood why our parents would risk everything to work here and start a new life.

But then I remembered: they never saw digis of Orbis. No one has, for that matter. It is forbidden to take or transmit digital images of any part of the rings. Stories and rumors and little bits from the Earth Seed Project provided the only basis for my parents' decision. They could never have seen this, let alone imagined it. And they never would, I suddenly realized.

Theylor was motioning for us to follow him. As he moved through the crowd, everyone stepped aside. Some dropped their heads, while others made strange gestures that made no sense to me. I followed along a channel, which was carved into the floor and filled with a light green liquid. Under my feet, aquatic aliens raced through the covered waterway to some unknown destination. Then Max bumped into a small alien that looked like it was made from liquid glass or maybe silicon. I watched Max's curiosity get the best of her as she poked the little alien. It squished under her fingers, and she reached out to touch the liquidlike creature again.

The alien cried out at Max. The sound was nothing more than clicks and hisses, but the creature seemed angry all the same.

"I'm sorry," I said, and pulled Max away. The being picked up little clear pieces of itself while still yelling at us.

"Did you see that?" she said. "Unbelievable."

"I know, but I can't understand a word," I said. "It's going to be hard."

"What about that thing Theylor mentioned? The trans —"

"The translation codec?"

"Yes. I want to get that," I said.

"Look at that one over there." Max pointed to a gaseous mix floating in the air. Little sparks of electricity flashed through the mist, and I could make out something I thought were eyes.

"Weird, isn't it?" I said.

"Wonderfully weird," Max said.

"Everything is so different."

"Not really," she said. "We have more in common with aliens than you think. We both find food and fluids for our bodies. We all sleep, communicate, have children, and group together to some extent. We're not that different."

Despite what Max said, it was obvious that we appeared very bizarre to the aliens. They all stopped and stared at us as we marched across the processing center, following Theylor. I guess it isn't every cycle that two hundred human children arrive on Orbis 1.

Theylor led us through an archway carved from a single piece of stone and into another chamber. Here, four more Keepers stood waiting, dwarfed by an oval window that ran the length of the enormous room. Through the window I could see the curved silhouette of Orbis 1 as it sparkled yellow, blue, and green.

The room was sparse: a few benches, which looked like they were made of crystal and metal, were scattered around, and a few odd-looking machines rested near the Keepers. That was it. But everything, including the intricate stone design on the polished floor, revealed the same attention to detail as the rest of the New Arrival Processing Center.

As we filed past, Theylor reached out and held me by the shoulder. Ketheria cowered toward Max. Theylor did not say a word; he just looked at me, tilting each of his heads. Then Theylor looked over at Ketheria, but she slipped behind Max.

"Did I do something wrong?" I asked him, but the alien only smiled and ran both of his large thin hands along the back of my head. What was he doing? It really gave me the creeps, but I didn't move. I just stared at the tracks of muscles and nerves visible under his bluish skin. He stared pretty hard at me, too. His eyes seemed like puddles of black oil.

After what seemed like an eternity, Theylor simply released me and nudged me toward the other children. No explanation at all.

"Now, that was weird," Theodore said.

"What do you think he was doing?" Max asked me.

"I have no idea."

The other Keepers methodically lined us up in front of the strange machines, each operated by a metallic robot. The bots were no more than two arms extending from the back of a comfortable-looking chair. Except this chair had a place to rest your face. Switzer bullied his way past most of the kids.

"Children," Theylor said, "everyone on Orbis receives the translation codec, or 'add-on,' if you like. We upload this to your neural storage membranes, and it allows you to translate what every inhabitant on the rings is saying."

"How do I upload something to my neural membranes?" Max interrupted.

"With your new neural synaptic hardware. The R5 here will implant the new device," Theylor replied.

"In my head?" Theodore said.

I looked at Max. She was equally shocked. We both looked at Ketheria. She was horrified. I knew one of the little ones would start crying at any moment.

"The process does not create pain. The

hardware will take a few minutes to work as the synthetic neurons make synaptic connections with your spinal cord. It will eventually make a connection with your optical nerve to assist in reading..."

That was enough. Two of the smaller children bolted for the door. Even Switzer stepped away from the machines and disappeared into the crowd. I looked for Ketheria, but she was gone.

"Joo'gh homm," one of the Keepers shouted.

This wasn't good. It would only fuel Switzer's argument.

"Do we need this codec?" I asked Theylor.

"You will understand nothing without it," he said. "This is part of living on Orbis."

"Theodore, you go first. Then the others will follow," I said.

"Me? No one's ever followed me," he replied.

I looked at Max. "Maybe you should go first. They *will* follow you," I said.

"I don't know about this," she argued.

"Please," I said, and chased after my sister.

Ketheria was quick. She had made it outside the processing room before I even got close to her. An alien with taut leathery skin and wide red eyes squawked at Ketheria when she bumped into him. Where she thought she was going, I had no idea. When I finally grabbed her shoulder, Ketheria thrashed about in my grip and would not open her eyes. I'd seen her do this many times while she slept in her nurture pod on the *Renaissance*.

"Ketheria. Ketheria! They're not going to hurt us. We're valuable to them." But Ketheria would not budge. "We have to do this. Everyone gets them."

A frail creature dressed completely in white stopped in front of Ketheria. Its skin glowed, and it gazed at Ketheria with big pupils of solid blue. The alien caressed Ketheria's forehead. My sister opened her eyes, but the alien did not say a thing. Then Ketheria smiled. The alien removed its hand and slipped away. Ketheria took my hand and led me back to the processing room.

"What did that alien do, Ketheria?" I looked back, but the crowd had consumed the alien. My sister just looked up and smiled.

When we returned to the processing room, several children were already showing off their new implants. The Keepers sat the kids with implants in front of displays that were similar to the O-dats on our ship but far simpler — just clear sheets of computerized silicon. Then one of the Keepers attached a thin clear cable to the neural port on each child.

When she was finished, Max got up and darted through the crowd. "It's nothin' — look!" She pulled her hair away, and just behind her right ear was a narrow black port, no more than a centimeter long. Max's skin was a little red, but she said, "I didn't feel a thing."

"Slaahn drot bahmneya te foolnum che mung," said one of the Keepers.

"What did he say?" I couldn't understand. It sounded like nothing more than vowels and tones with the occasional throat noise for emphasis.

"Ha! He didn't understand him. I did," Max said to another girl. "I already uploaded my translation codec."

Ketheria and I were in line and slowly moving toward the R5. One appendage of the bot braced the person against the seat while the other administered the hardware.

"Amazing technology!" I heard Max say behind me.

The only thing I heard coming from the Keepers' mouths were weird sounds. They were directing the children with the new hardware, who obviously knew exactly what the Keepers were saying. I admit, I was eager to get mine.

Ketheria was next. She was no longer afraid. Whatever that alien had done, it worked. Before Ketheria took her seat in front of the R5, Theylor was back. He took me by the shoulder again.

"Please, come with me."

"But my sister. I —"

"She will be fine now," Theylor said as he led me to one of the empty O-dats. "Take a seat please."

Am I in trouble? I wondered. Nervous, I followed his instructions. *Do they know about the files I took?* That would be impossible. I wanted my implant.

"Johnny, I want you to —"

"How do you know my name?"

"I know a lot about things, as you will soon discover," Theylor said. "Now please face the screen." A few of the other children gathered around. "I want you to concentrate on the screen. Without touching the screen, I want you to scroll through the files."

"That's easy," I told him. "Anyone can do that."

"Yeah, right," Switzer said, now standing behind me.

I scrolled through the files without touching the screen. This was something I always did. I thought everyone could do it.

"Johnny," Theylor said, "I want you to locate a file named Translation Codec. The computer will automatically compensate for your language."

"What do you mean?" I said.

"Do not think. Feel. Grasp the file with your mind. Visualize it in the front of your forehead — like one of these displays. Make it part of yourself."

I thought about the file, and there it was on the O-dat. Usually I just asked Mother for something like that.

"Now I want you to scan the file and store it in your memory."

"He can't do that," Switzer said.

"Yeah, Theylor, he's right," I said — although I hated to admit that Switzer could be right about anything. "I don't think I can do that." Max came to my side. Ketheria was there also. A lot of people were gawking at me now.

I didn't know how to scan a file with my mind.

What was I supposed to do? I looked harder, but nothing happened. "I don't get this," I told Theylor. "Why can't I just have my implant?"

"Concentrate," he said.

I thought of the file opening up. I pictured it jumping into my brain. I felt silly.

"I can't do it, Theylor."

"See?" Theylor said. "You should find this very easy."

"But I didn't do anything," I said.

"I am speaking to you right now in my own language," he said. His lips moved slightly out of sync with his speech. "You understand what I'm saying, do you not?" I nodded. His pronunciation was much clearer, too.

"What did double-dome just say?" Switzer asked. Obviously he had not received his implant yet.

"JT, you can upload the files with your mind!" Theodore said.

"That's so awesome!" Max said.

"You are a *softwire*," Theylor announced.

"A what?"

"A softwire. I have never known of this ability in the human species, but you *are* a softwire."

"What does that mean?" I asked. The crowd was getting louder and larger. Now the other Keepers joined in also.

"It means that you can access any computer by simply standing near it. Many computers transmit data back and forth. You are able to access this stream and the data within a computer without any additional hardware. You do not need the implant. That is how you could talk to Mother on your seedship."

How does he know about that? I wondered.

"I told you he was telling the truth," Max said to Switzer.

"Hmmf," was his only reply.

"Are there any others?" I asked. I didn't want to be the only one again. I had lived with being different for thirteen years on the *Renaissance*.

"There are none on Orbis," Theylor said. "Although softwires are extremely rare, all Space Jumpers are softwires."

A few in the crowd whispered. I had read about Space Jumpers on the *Renaissance*. An odd, raw-edged sort of panic caught hold of me. *I don't want to be a Space Jumper,* I thought. *I just want the implant. I want to be like everyone else for a change.*

"Everyone, we must continue with the arrival process," Theylor said. "Please get back in line if you have not received your implant."

"If he can do that, then so can I," Switzer declared, and sat at the screen. He scrunched his eyes and concentrated on the file.

"Come now, please. Your implant will be sufficient," Theylor said, and gently nudged him.

Switzer slammed the table and stood up.

"It's pretty awesome you're a softwire," Theodore said. "Did you know?"

"Not a clue. Well, there was the whole Mother

thing."

"I wonder what it means. You know, to be the first human softwire."

I didn't have a response for him before Max slipped into our conversation. "I wonder what other things you can do. I can't wait to try it out," Max said, and smiled.

I looked at Theodore, but he just shrugged. Max seemed pretty comfortable with me now as she reached up and searched behind my ear where the implant should be. She was already planning on taking something apart.

"Hey, stop that," I told her.

I turned my attention to Switzer, who was finally getting his implant. The R5 pushed Switzer's face into the chair and inserted the implant. Switzer got up scowling and rubbed behind his ear. He brushed past me and whispered, "Freak." But I just turned away. I wondered how my newfound gift would be received on Orbis.

Once all of the other kids had received their neural implants, Theylor guided us back through the New Arrival Processing's main lobby. With my new translation codec and a little help from the central computer, I was able to understand everything the other aliens were saying. Tall ones, small ones, even really weird ones all spoke in a language I could understand. But I wasn't listening. I was thinking about Theylor's revelation.

A softwire? Space Jumpers? Everyone knew that

Space Jumpers were fearless humanoids who slipped through space and time. We had read all about them on the *Renaissance*. Space Jumpers had roamed the rings since the Ancients controlled Orbis, and they were the elite force that protected the Keepers against the First Families during the War of Ten Thousand Rotations. But the Citizens, most of them descendants of the First Families, still feared the Space Jumpers and had forced the Keepers to banish them from the rings almost a thousand years ago. How could I possibly have anything in common with them?

"Excuse me," Max said as she maneuvered around a small dusty alien that looked as though it had just come out of the ground.

"You excuse me! You surface dwellers think you can walk wherever you want. Well, I'm standing here right now. It's not often I'm aboveground, so please let me stand here."

The alien sucked in as much air as its crusty little body could hold. It looked quite angry, puffing up in front of Max in an attempt to look threatening.

"The aliens understand you now also," said Theylor, who came up from behind and stood in front of the alien. "Their codec translates your language to theirs, but it does not translate gestures, cultural differences, or *manners.* " Theylor glared at the alien, who shriveled back down. "For that, you will attend social classes."

Theylor led us away from the enraged alien and across the atrium to a large tubelike passage.

"Children, gather around, please."

We circled around Theylor. Ketheria was at my side.

"We will now proceed to the assignment sector. We will board the spaceway for transportation to the other side of Orbis 1, where you will meet your new Guarantor."

When Theylor finished talking, the tube filled with a sleek transportation device that looked a lot like a monorail. The large doors of the metal vehicle slid up, and we all followed the Keeper onto the spaceway. I sat in one of the many seats, and it immediately shifted and conformed to the shape of my body. Two armrests emerged at my sides, and I ran my hands along the smooth, polished material. *Is everything this nice on Orbis?* I wondered.

"A gravity cushion will hold you in place," Theylor said. "Once the spaceway reaches the outside of the ring, you will be in zero gravity. Without the cushion, I am afraid your ride would not be very comfortable."

The monorail slid into outer space, clinging tightly to the shell of Orbis 1. I felt something push down on my body, an invisible force that kept me in my seat. It must have been the gravity cushion. I glanced at Max. She was laughing again, looking around to see where the force was coming from.

Then the floor of the spaceway appeared to fade away beneath my feet. Everyone gasped at the illusion. I saw Theodore tap his toe on the floor to see if it was still there. I noticed Theylor staring through the floor at the moons, Ki and Ta.

"Orbis certainly is a beautiful place, Theylor," I said, trying to start a conversation.

"The crystal moons have been very fruitful for us," replied Theylor's left head while his right remained fixed on the moons.

"I'm surprised more people — I mean, you know . . . other species — don't try to come here," I whispered to him.

"Oh, they do, but it is not allowed. Population control is an important part of our work here, along with protecting the sanctity of our moons."

"Theylor, can I ask you a question?"

"You are free to ask anything you like, Johnny Turnbull."

"What happened when we arrived? Did something go wrong with the central computer?"

Theylor did not respond right away. I thought maybe I'd hit a sore spot.

"Theylor?"

Theylor turned both heads toward me. "There is nothing to worry about now, but you must understand something. The central computer is a brilliant and magnificent machine. It is a necessity to our life on Orbis. More so than even the oxygen you need to stay alive."

"Like Mother was on the *Renaissance*," I said.

"Yes, and more. If Mother had failed on your journey, you would not be sitting across from me right now," Theylor said. "If the central computer failed, neither of us would be sitting here." He paused. "Our existence depends on the central computer. The Ancients spent much time and energy in building it. Some of the technology is still a mystery to us to this day. The central computer self-corrected the event that happened when you arrived, but the fact that the event happened at all is still very disturbing to some."

Theylor turned both heads back to the moons. There was a lot I wanted to learn about my new home, especially about the central computer, but I sensed the conversation was over.

4

The trip on the spaceway was quick. The ride through zero gravity let the transport travel at great velocities. Once the monorail passed back through the ring, gravity returned to normal.

"Children, stay together now. We will cross through the Trading Hall, where you will be assigned your Guarantor."

As we followed Theylor off the spaceway, some of the other kids gathered around me.

"Couldn't you tell you were a softwire?" asked one girl who had never spoken to me on the *Renaissance*.

"How?" I replied.

"But you knew you could move files around just by thinking about it," she said.

"I thought that was normal. I used to think speaking to Mother was normal," I said, not accustomed to this much attention. I always kept to myself on the *Renaissance*. It felt odd discussing my newfound ability in front of everyone.

"Well, I'm glad they discovered that you're a softwire," Max said so everyone heard. "Makes us humans look a little more important, don't you think?"

I heard Switzer scoff.

The Trading Hall spaceway station was nothing

like New Arrival Processing. Flashing lights, booming announcements, and strange aromas of alien spices overloaded my senses. I walked with Theylor past brilliant O-dats that towered above me, advertising everything from private space shuttles to boots and even neural-port enhancements (whatever those were). Each vendor tried to upstage the next one. Holographic 3-D salespeople floated overhead, begging us to visit their trading chamber. I even saw a 3-D holograph passing out electronic paper to Theodore. He stood staring at the handout.

"How could he do that? He's a holograph," Theodore said.

"Children, we need to get through here quickly," Theylor said. "We are about to go outside."

I followed Theylor through the atrium doors. The crisp air caught me by surprise. Then it hit me. I'd never been *outside* before.

"Whoa," Max said as she stood in the open air and looked up.

I followed her gaze. The effect was dizzying. I reached for something to steady myself with — anything.

"I'm gonna fall," Theodore said, and sat on the ground.

The ring curled up and over my head. The stars were still visible toward the edges of the ring, and the atmosphere hung thick and dark, tinted with a greenish blue the color of hydraulic fluid.

Something didn't look right. My mind was wandering. I wasn't thinking straight. *You need to sit down,* I told myself.

Theylor stood there watching us. "I should have anticipated this," he said. "You have lived your entire lives under a ceiling. Take a moment to orient yourselves. This effect will diminish."

I took deep breaths. The oxygen was thinner than on the ship or in the atrium. I looked around. The effect was the same on everyone.

"You all right?" I said to my sister. "What is it, Ketheria?"

She nodded and pointed above my head. I looked up and saw a tree, a beautiful, regal tree. I reached around and ran my hand along the trunk. Ketheria did the same. So did Max and Theodore.

"Please, children, if you are ready, we must proceed this way," Theylor pleaded.

But this was a tree. A real tree. I had never seen one before. Yes, I'd seen digis of trees, but never one planted right in front of me.

"It's so tall," one boy said.

"I like the roughness," another said.

Ketheria was right against the tree. She leaned her whole body against it and closed her eyes.

"Theylor?" came a voice behind us. I turned around and saw another Keeper marching across the garden. His gait was confident; his eyes focused on Theylor. "Why are these children not assigned yet? Their Guarantors grow impatient."

His voice was steely and sharp. Nothing like

Theylor's. He was dressed in a purple robe, just like the other Keepers, but he carried himself with the same arrogance as Switzer.

"Children, let me introduce you to Drapling. He assists the Guarantors and the Trading Council with their new arrivals," Theylor said.

"*Acquisitions* is the proper term," Drapling corrected as he scanned the group.

Even though Theylor's eyes were creepy, they still seemed deep and warm, almost comforting. But Drapling's were the exact opposite. I could see fire rumbling behind them. The intensity withered his skin and made his foreheads scowl. I figured Drapling was someone to stay away from.

"I need every last one of you in the assignment sector now . . . *please*," Drapling said. Theylor bowed his heads and did not interrupt.

Drapling turned his right head to Theylor and said, "Show me the Softwire."

"Johnny, come here, please," Theylor said.

How does this Keeper know about me already? I wondered.

"A human softwire. Well, what a very big day for your species. I know of no other human with this ability. I'm sure your Guarantor will feel better for having to take care of a bunch of children." Drapling then spoke to the whole group. "By decree set forth by the Keepers, the Trading Council, which arranged passage for your parents, must now take responsibility for your well-being."

"As slaves!" Switzer interrupted.

"If you define slavery as working for your parents' honor, as well as your keep, then, yes, as slaves. Most Guarantors are not happy about this situation, either. Instead of a shipful of adult workers, they must settle for a small cargo of unskilled children. But they will follow the orders of the Keepers, as will all of you. Now follow me . . . please."

I had forgotten about Ketheria. She was still wrapped around the tree and had completely ignored Drapling's request. As the other children filed past Drapling, I watched the Keeper turn and head straight for Ketheria. The determination in his stride made me feel that something bad was about to happen. I could not let him get ahold of my sister. I needed to do something, quick. I stepped in front of him.

"Drapling, what if I don't want a Guarantor? What if I want to be on my own?" I asked.

That worked. Drapling stopped in midstride. Actually, everyone stopped.

"I wouldn't choose this moment to get brave, JT," Theodore said.

"There are many things you do not know, young human, such as the consequence we impose on those who do not follow the decrees set forth by the Keepers." Drapling leaned in lower. He whispered now. "Break the decree and you just might wish you had died along with your parents."

I barely heard what Drapling said. I was concerned only with my sister's safety.

"Step out of my way," Drapling demanded.

But I couldn't. I couldn't even glance back at her for fear I would tip Drapling off. *Move, Ketheria. Get back in line.*

"Do you not hear me, Softwire?"

"Yes," I said, "I understand." I closed my eyes and stepped aside.

Drapling turned his attention back to Ketheria, but she was gone, safely hidden among the other children now filing into the Assignment Sector.

The Assignment Sector was even larger than the chamber at the New Arrival Processing Center. *How big is this place?* I wondered as Theylor guided us toward a ramp at the edge of the round room.

"Follow this to the stage at the far end," Theylor said, pointing toward an area illuminated by an enormous pulsing teardrop of glass.

"Come here, Ketheria," I said, and took her hand. Together we crossed the narrow riser, staying clear of the blue electrical fence that penned us in.

At our feet, running the entire length of the riser, stood a collection of aliens, who began pointing and whispering as we paraded past them.

"Is that fence for us or them?" Theodore said.

I stared down to the end of the riser, searching between the pulses of light to catch a glimpse of what they had in store for us. But whoever stood there waiting was concealed by the garish light, and I could only make out silhouettes against the tall, narrow windows that curved over the auditorium.

The riser opened onto a round stage big enough for all of us and then some. The electrical charge from the fence collected in a channel that encircled the entire area. Standing on the other side were four Keepers, now joined by Theylor and Drapling. Past them, waiting on a raised area made of stone and decorated with metal and crystal, was another group of aliens. They stared at us eagerly, as if sizing us up for something important. *Are these our Guarantors?* I wondered. My eyes darted from alien to alien, and I noticed that most of them flaunted some item bearing the insignia of Orbis. Whether it was a large belt or a necklace, a pin, or even a crown, each displayed the same symbol — four overlapping rings around a glowing light.

"Trusted Citizens," Drapling announced, "we have your consignments."

"So we belong to these guys now?" Theodore whispered. I knew only Citizens could be Guarantors. "I guess so," I said.

"Drapling, I want the Softwire," grumbled one unusually large Citizen. His legs alone were six or seven times the width of my whole body. Perched on top of his massive light yellow form was a small pea-size face. At least twenty wires protruded from his skull and connected to a silver spherical device floating above his tiny head.

"How do they know about you already?" Theodore whispered.

"I think the central computer must have alerted them."

"Why should you get the Softwire, Boohral?" said another Guarantor, jutting what might have passed for a chin toward the smooth, pale yellow giant. This Guarantor looked much older, with an abundance of wrinkled pink skin. His eyes drooped around the side of his head, and there was a large, clear bubble of skin on his forehead that changed color when he talked.

Boohral's two assistants immediately struck an aggressive stance in front of the other Guarantor. The assistants wore vests matching the color of Boohral's belt. I thought they might be Boohral's bodyguards, but from the frightened expressions on their long faces, I knew they did not want to fight.

"Because, Torlee, there are certain Citizens who should not possess such an instrument," Boohral said.

"Are you accusing me of something?" demanded Torlee, the fleshy globe on his head flushing a deep red.

"Enough with the ridiculous bickering!" Drapling shouted. "The assignments were made many years ago, before some of you were even involved. We will keep to the original agreements or you will forfeit your claims," ordered Drapling.

"But we did not know there was a softwire on board!" Boohral shouted. "I demand a hearing before the Trading Council."

But before Drapling could respond, Theylor spoke up and said, "Friends, please. This is an insignificant event. It does not require the valuable time of the Trading Council. The decree set by the Keepers cannot be changed. The Trading Council has agreed to commit to the cargo and we must disperse them."

"Do not confuse this with a load of Greepling feed from Tristan," Drapling said, his voice filled with contempt.

"Nor do I consider it a load of ordinary humans, either," said another Guarantor with insectlike antennas. "How do we know there are not more softwires?"

The Guarantors grumbled to each other, and the atmosphere grew more and more intense. Boohral appeared to be gaining support.

Theylor raised his arms to quiet the crowd. "I assure you, every human was checked. There is only one," he said.

"I'll find it," Boohral announced, and he pushed his way through the other aliens. The huge Guarantor labored toward a ramp at the end of the stone riser. A few of the children moved away from me as Boohral reached the open area where the Keepers stood. Theylor raised his hand, and the massive alien froze on the spot. I don't think he could have moved even if he had wanted to.

"Engage the protector shield around the children," Theylor said.

Drapling walked over to us. "This is for your own protection, but do not touch the barrier."

With that, Drapling tapped on a portable O-dat molded to his wrist. The channel in the floor began to glow around us, and a force field shot up, surrounding us completely. A few of the kids gasped.

"Convene the Council," Drapling ordered.

We sat and waited while the Keepers contacted the members of the Trading Council, all twelve of them. I overheard that some members were on other rings, while others were on the moons. A few members were even in distant galaxies. Five members attended the meeting only as holographic projections — larger-than-life three-dimensional representations that paced through the great hall above everyone's heads. One of the projections was hunched over, talking intently with Torlee, whose head-bubble kept changing color. I noticed Boohral scrutinizing them from the corner of his eye.

"Now," Drapling announced, "we will begin."

One of the holographs stepped forward. "Which one of you has chosen to question the decree of the Keepers?"

"I have," Boohral said.

"Ah, Boohral. You are always trying to change the deal," said the Trading Council member.

"The deal changed. I did not. We were never told of the Softwire."

"Nor were we, Boohral," said the Trading Council member who had been talking to Torlee. She had jet-black skin and piercing silver eyes. "The deceased human cargo was not supposed to bring offspring. They broke this rule by storing embryos

— embryos they planned to birth late in the journey. When the adults died from an unknown malfunction on the spacecraft, there wasn't any knowledge of the unborn, let alone the existence of a softwire."

"How do you know this?" demanded Boohral.

I wondered the same thing.

"Their ship is in our control now," she said. "I personally searched the ship's AI. There is nothing we don't know," she said.

I thought about my parents' restricted files. Did they know about those, too?

The Trading Council member looked like a human, but I could not tell where her skin stopped and her leathery outfit began. Her pure white hair was braided. Strands of it hung in front of her face, while the rest lay obediently against her ebony skull.

"We learned that one of the children was a softwire only when the Keeper tried to install the implant. Theylor suspected the male's abilities and ran the tests with the central computer. It was only then that the central computer notified us of the event. No one has tried to cheat anyone. The decree stands."

Our Guarantors grumbled and thumped on the riser.

"Silence!" shouted the Council member.

"But Madame Lee, it is we who must bear the financial burden!" said a knobby, crusted Guarantor.

"Yes, Weegin, that is true," Madame Lee replied.

"But why?" demanded Boohral.

Drapling stepped in and said, "As Citizens, you have chosen to stock your factories with knudniks, as you like to call them. Therefore you should bear the responsibility in matters like this."

Boohral hissed in response. In fact, most of the Guarantors either grunted or scoffed at Drapling's answer.

I leaned in to Max. "What's a knudnik?" I said.

"I don't know, but you've suddenly gotten very popular. I'm glad you're the one with the softy thing and not me."

"See, I told you he was a freak," Switzer said. He worked his way through the other children and stood next to Ketheria. She stuck her tongue out at him.

"Please. Everyone calm down," Theylor said. "The honorable Trading Council member has spoken. Madame Lee has upheld the decree of the Keepers, and rightly so."

"A concession should be made to the Guarantors who do not receive the Softwire," said the alien with the antennas.

"Speak up," Boohral urged the alien. Drapling twisted his left head, and anger boiled in his eyes. I don't think he was used to compromising with anyone.

"The Softwire has a sibling. Maybe the sister can go to another Guarantor and we can see if this evolutionary break shows up in her," said Torlee.

"But who decides which of us gets the female?" Boohral asked.

Did I hear right? Split us up? This cannot be happening. I grabbed Ketheria with no intention of letting go.

"This would be an easy solution to our problem," Madame Lee said. "But the Keeper's decree is never to break up families. You know the laws."

"I don't care about human beings!" Boohral yelled. "You care only because you smell like one. You have sympathy for these weak, pathetic creatures — everyone knows it!"

Madame Lee stood tall, deflecting the full brunt of the insult. Several Citizens moved away from Boohral, and everyone whispered frantically. Then Madame Lee's 3-D holograph appeared instantly in front of Boohral and sprang taller, immediately towering over him. Boohral's two assistants stepped in front of him as a glowing blue disc materialized in Madame Lee's right hand. She hurled the disc at the assistants. Boohral didn't even flinch. One assistant ducked, moving out of the way just in time. But then the disc turned back, striking the assistant in the back of the head, killing him instantly.

I shuddered in disbelief. This was the first time I had ever seen someone be killed. Instinctively I stood in front of Ketheria. I watched in horror as two small droids lifted the broken body of the assistant into a glass-and-metal coffin. The coffin filled with blue gas as the robots took it away.

"How dare you disrespect these proceedings!" Drapling fumed.

"How is that possible? She's only a holograph," Theodore whispered to me.

"You will pay for my loss," Boohral demanded.

"Be thankful it was not you," Madame Lee said.

"I am far too profitable to the Council. Your threats are empty," Boohral said.

"I do not care for Trefaldoors like yourself, Boohral, despite your business skills. Remember your place. If you ever address me in this manner again, I will send you through the wormhole where they eat fat Trefaldoors for —"

They completely ignored Drapling, which only made him angrier. "The deconstructive energy you released by your killing is an affront to the Ancients. How dare you —"

"Everyone, please, this has gotten out of hand," Theylor said as he stepped between Drapling and the hologram of Madame Lee. Boohral moved away.

"I am sorry, Madame Lee, but you will be charged for Boohral's loss if he decides to initiate a demand of payment," Theylor announced while staring at Drapling with one head. The other Keepers scurried about, seemingly distraught by Drapling's outburst. "Boohral, do you desire to initiate a demand of payment for the destruction of your property?"

"Absolutely," he replied.

"Then, Madame Lee, by order —"

"Bah!" Before Theylor could finish, Madame Lee threw a fistful of crystals at Boohral's feet. They sparked as they entered our realm. The remaining assistant scurried to pick them up.

"We have made a decision," said a Trading Council member with a long tail and feet like a centipede's. "The Guarantor that receives the Softwire will forfeit one child to each of the other Guarantors. If he does not want to do this, he can forfeit the Softwire to the next Guarantor, who then has the same choice." With that, the Trading Council member rang a chime and each of the members either left or blinked off.

"That's not fair. Now I will have an extra mouth to feed," said one of the Guarantors.

"And an extra pair of hands to charge a fee for," Drapling said with a sneer, and Theylor once again glanced in his direction.

"Ah, what can they earn for me?" Torlee mumbled. "We should have turned the ship back."

The force field dropped into the floor again. Theylor motioned us to the center of the room, but no one moved.

"It is all right," Theylor said. "Come now."

I stepped forward first, along with Ketheria, then Max and Switzer followed. Slowly, the other children began to move. The stone riser slid away from us, revealing a semicircle of crystal orbs embedded in the floor.

"Quiet, please. When I call out your name, please move behind the Guarantor I direct you to," Theylor said.

The Guarantors circled around us. Their assistants stayed behind.

"How's this going to work?" I said to Theodore.

"Eight Guarantors. Two hundred of us. That's twenty-five for each Guarantor, and whoever gets you has to give up seven," he quickly replied.

I didn't care about the math. I hoped this meant that Switzer would finally be out of my life. Slave or not, any sort of existence would be easier without him. One by one, the Guarantors stepped onto the flattened crystal orbs. The orb under each Guarantor changed to a different color.

The process was very quick. Max, Ketheria, and I were all assigned to the same Guarantor — the cragged little alien named Weegin, with the beady red eyes and tough, wrinkled skin. The alien was caressing a white puffy larva in his hands as kids I rarely spoke with lined up behind the other Guarantors.

"Theodore Malone!" Theylor called out, and then pointed to Weegin. "You are assigned to Joca Krig Weegin."

"Randall Switzer!" Theylor called next. *Please let him go somewhere else,* I thought. But Theylor pointed and said, "Also Joca Krig Weegin."

Who was punishing me like this? What were the odds? Switzer looked at me and smirked. Orbis would be no different from the *Renaissance* — I just knew it. I looked at the kids standing around Weegin. At least I had Theodore, I told myself, and Max, too.

"Who has the Softwire?" Boohral asked when Theylor was finished.

"Joca Krig Weegin does," Theylor said.

Boohral made a loud clicking noise with his mouth. It was obvious that he was angry.

"Joca Krig Weegin, do you wish to keep the Softwire?" Drapling asked.

"Most definitely," my new Guarantor replied.

"Argh! Come, humans." Boohral was gathering his bounty and leaving.

"Do you not want your compensation?" Drapling asked.

"Make it quick."

"Joca Krig Weegin, please assign one child to each of the other Guarantors. Do not separate the Softwire from his sibling."

This was my chance. Weegin began pulling children from the group one by one. *Take Switzer*, I pleaded silently.

But he was weeding out the smallest kids first. "These are no good to me," he said, adding to my feeling that I was nothing more than cargo to him.

When Ketheria was the only little one left, Weegin sent an other girl over to Torlee, who was still scowling about not getting me, the Softwire. Another boy, whom I had played Quest-Nest with many times in the contest tank, went with the only human-looking Guarantor. But Switzer was still with us. *Why can't he get rid of Switzer?* If there ever was someone I wanted to go, it was Switzer.

"One more, Weegin," Drapling said.

"Give me a good one," Boohral said.

Weegin looked at Switzer.

Yes.

But then Weegin grabbed Max by the collar instead.

"No, please," Max said.

I immediately stood in front of Max. "No, take him," I said, and pointed to Switzer.

"Don't want to lose your new girlfriend?" Switzer said with a sneer.

Max took a swing at Switzer.

"She'll do fine," growled Boohral.

"Do as you're told," Weegin snapped in a foul, crusty tone.

"No!" I yelled.

Ketheria's eyes welled up. I looked at Max. "Don't worry. I'll find out where you live."

"Move, human," Weegin growled.

"Watch out for Switzer," she whispered, swallowing hard and holding back tears. She bent down and kissed Ketheria on the cheek — an Earth gesture we had picked up from the movies. She headed to her new Guarantor — the fat yellow one with wires sticking out of his head. Boohral grabbed Max by the shoulder and pushed her in with the rest of the children. I watched as Max left the hall. Ketheria fought to hold her tears back, but many other children were not that strong. I felt my stomach rip away. I wanted to throw up. I wanted to cry, too, to scream out loud, but I wouldn't dare let anyone see that, especially Switzer. I swallowed back my tears, stood tall, and took Ketheria's hand. *Not a good start,* I thought.

5

All those years on the *Renaissance* and never once had I imagined my life would be like this. Max and most of the other kids were gone and I didn't know if I would ever see them again. My softwire ability made me the center of much unwanted attention. Sure, now the other kids knew I wasn't crazy when I said I could talk to Mother, and the thing that made me feel different had a name — I was a softwire. But I was still different, and now that Mother was gone, I felt more alone than ever.

The death of Boohral's assistant flashed through my mind again and again as I rode on the spaceway with my new Guarantor. Would anyone ever initiate demand for payment for the destruction of me or Ketheria, or Theodore even? I was shocked at how casually Madame Lee had destroyed life. I made a point of remembering that. I also made a point to remember to be very careful in my new surroundings.

No one spoke for the entire ride on the spaceway, or the tram ride through a construction zone buzzing with flying robots, or the short walk to the huge structure that I assumed was our new home.

"This is Weegin's World!" exclaimed our Guarantor, still caressing the infant larva in his hand. "Everyone, stay close to me."

We followed Weegin into the mouth of a

windowless metallic building and down a hallway. Weegin stopped in front of two large glass doors.

"Cover your ears. It can get loud," Weegin said. "And don't touch anything. I don't want to lose any of you on the first day."

"Better watch it, freak," Switzer said, bumping into my shoulder, but I didn't even bother to reply. On Orbis, Switzer was quickly becoming the least of my worries.

I grabbed Ketheria's hand as we entered the guts of Weegin's World, a cavernous dome-within-a-dome filled with machines, grease, and dirt. In contrast to the luxury we had witnessed earlier, our new home was ugly. It seemed that our Guarantor spent his fortunes on machinery, not comforts. Under the metallic dome, enormous robotic cranes tossed around cargo containers as if they were toy blocks. Tentacles from the massive cranes gripped the inner dome for support while these metal monsters plucked cargo through the giant energy field that pierced the skin of the outer dome. The enormous claws deposited the containers for smaller robots to crack open and sort their contents, which were more containers. The whole process looked to me like some absurd ballet. *Max would love to see this,* I thought.

Weegin piled us into a lift that took us high over the factory. The air was stale and smelled of grease, just like the manufacturing corridor on our seed-ship. Weegin ignited a bright green energy field that served as a walkway over the entire workings of

Weegin's World.

"I'm a jobber," Weegin said. "Look over here." We leaned against the railing to see where he was pointing. "Every time a starship is forfeited, I put in a bid for its cargo with the Trading Council. Anytime a vendor goes out of business — even in other star systems — I buy their stock. I grab whatever I can find."

"You collect junk," Switzer said.

Weegin grabbed Switzer by the nose and twisted it. Switzer cried out in pain. Weegin, who was quite strong for his size, dragged Switzer to the front of the group.

"Is this junk?" Weegin asked, referring to us. "I don't think you would call your friends junk."

"Maybe," he said.

Weegin twisted harder.

"Yer gonna rip my nose off!" Switzer cried.

Weegin pushed him to the floor. Switzer massaged his nose, which was already swelling up.

"Jobbing is how I acquired you. Just prior to your arrival, when the Keepers announced the death of your crew, a few companies forfeited their claims. That's when I put in a bid, and now I have you." Weegin looked straight into my eyes.

"What are we supposed to do?" asked a girl named Grace.

Weegin moved down the overhead railing to another glass door.

"Depends on you and how smart you are," he replied.

Weegin picked up a scrap of metal and threw it onto the floor. Instantly, small robotic scavengers scurried across the factory floor and devoured the scrap.

"Just don't get in the way of those critters." He chuckled. "Some of you," Weegin continued, "will process inventory data, while most of you will sort the smaller bins the robots are too clumsy to handle. A lot of small stuff has big payout."

Weegin piled us into another lift, which went even higher. He focused his beady eyes on me and added, "I'm interested to see what you can do. You better be worth it."

The elevator opened into a small round room. There was nothing in the room except for some vestlike garments hanging on the walls — some small, some bigger, but all of them deep blue in color.

"Every one of you must wear one of these skins." Weegin held one up for everyone to see. "This skin tells everyone you belong to me. Once you put it on, you are never to leave Weegin's World without it. Matter of fact, you are never allowed to leave your room without it, or you will not get back in."

Weegin turned and waved the vest over the sensor near the door. The door disappeared. I noticed two bones extending from Weegin's back and through the thick material of his shirt. The bones were jagged on the ends, as if someone had snapped something off them.

"The skin is electronically programmed to open any door you are authorized to go through. Your own skin will open the door to your quarters. Only your quarters. Find one that fits," Weegin said, "and follow me."

I reached for a skin, but Switzer, whose nose was now purple and swollen, snatched it away.

"The girls' skins are on the other side," Switzer said.

"Nice nose, by the way," I said. I grabbed the next skin and slid my arms through the holes.

The skin clamped around me. It was more metal than fabric. I held up my arms and twisted. The vest resisted slightly.

"Every time you forget your skin and I have to let you in, that will cost you two chits. If you lose your skin, that will cost you thirty chits, so don't lose it. If you break a rule, that will cost anywhere from one chit to fifty chits, maybe more...."

"What's a chit?" I said.

Weegin whirled around. "Did they not tell you anything about the ring?"

"A little bit," I said, following Weegin down the hallway.

"Against the wishes of the Trading Council, you are paid for your services with chits," he said.

This was good, I thought. It wasn't slavery after all. I would have money. I could buy things and maybe have a real life yet.

"You are charged three chits every phase for your sleeper. An extra chit for clean sheets — which

I enforce, by the way. I don't want you humans stinking up Weegin's World. Meals are two chits a phase — that's all the Keepers let me charge. I don't know how they expect me to feed you on two chits a phase." Weegin was rambling. "Anyway, there's a chit charge for —"

"Weegin," I interrupted, "how much do we get paid to help you as jobbers?"

"Two chits per work spoke," Weegin snapped. "More than you're worth."

I knew four spokes made one cycle and four cycles made a phase. Four phases made a set, and ten sets made one rotation.

I knew a rotation on Orbis was like a year on Earth. "How many spokes do we have to work?" I asked.

"I can make you work only one spoke per cycle," Weegin answered.

Two chits per work spoke meant eight chits per phase. With the cost of room and board . . . that left me with two chits a phase if I didn't break any of Weegin's rules. I didn't know how much a chit was, but I assumed financial independence was now out the window.

Weegin stopped in a small foyer at the end of a lofty hall and removed a small electronic device from a belt on his hip. He waved it over Grace's implant and then the vest. "One spoke of each cycle is for recreation and chores. Don't forget your chores. Why you need a spoke for recreation is beyond my comprehension. You are not here for fun. Fun is not an option at Weegin's World." He moved Grace aside as the lift rose along the corridor, then he reached for another child. "One spoke is for social studies and one spoke is for sleep." Weegin continued brushing the device over each child. "I'm programming your implants and your skins with your room assignment. We have found sleepers similar to the ones on your seedship." We all stopped in front of another lift. "Step onto the lift and it will take you to your room. The door will automatically admit your entry."

"I don't have an implant," I told Weegin.

"Do you think I'm stupid?" he said with a snarl.

"No, I mean I just —"

"I'm aware of what you have and don't have. It shouldn't matter, if you are what they say."

Weegin waved the wand where my implant would have been and shrugged his leathery shoulders. The two thick bones poking out of his back twitched in unison.

"Females first onto the lift," Weegin ordered.

I was staring at the sharp spikes that seemed to grow from Weegin's temples when Ketheria grabbed my arm.

"Don't worry, Ketheria, I'll just be down the hall. Besides, I couldn't leave even if I wanted to," I said, tugging at my vest.

Ketheria only held on tighter. She wouldn't let go. Grace came up behind us.

"Well, Ketheria, I guess we're roommates," she said.

"See?" I said to Ketheria. I gently tried to pry her fingers from my arm. "Grace will be here with you, and you can come see me whenever you want."

Grace reached out and took Ketheria's hand. "Go — it'll be fine."

Ketheria's grip loosened, and she let Grace lead her onto the lift. But her eyes never left mine. Even though she didn't say anything, somehow I knew what she was feeling — neither of us wanted to be separated. When Ketheria finally looked away, I boarded another lift, one of at least twenty that skimmed the outer walls. I watched Ketheria's lift stop in front of her room. A little farther down, my lift stopped and an opening appeared in the seamless metal wall.

"I guess this is home," I said.

Switzer pushed past me. "Get out of the way, roomie."

"This is your room, too?"

"Better get used to it, freak."

I followed Switzer inside the small, narrow room. The smell of grease was just as dreadful as in the factory. There were lockers on both sides and a simple door at the far end. I waited for Switzer to choose a locker, and then I selected one on the other side of the room. Inside I found some clothes, some sort of light source, clean sheets for my sleeper, and a pair of used work boots.

"I wonder where Weegin found these," I said, holding the boots up.

"What do you care?" Switzer said as he headed for the door, which disappeared when he stood in front of it.

The next room contained four sleepers and nothing else. It seemed that our provisions barely exceeded the minimums required by the Keepers. The sleepers looked different from the ones on our seed-ship. These were built into the walls and stacked one on top of another. I figured Switzer would try to take any sleeper I took interest in, so I stood next to the sleeper farthest from the door. Switzer pushed me out of the way.

"That one's mine," he said, right on cue.

That was easy. I turned and took the top sleeper near the door, just in case Ketheria needed me.

Dalton Billings entered the room behind Theodore. "We have to sleep with them?" he said to Switzer.

He took the sleeper under Switzer, while Theodore immediately grabbed the sleeper under mine. Sides were drawn once again. This felt familiar. I was afraid of Switzer, but I would never admit it. He would use my fear against me. On the *Renaissance* I had avoided him and lived in the shadows. I did not want to do that here. I decided right then and there that I would not live that way on Orbis. Somehow I would have the life I dreamed of.

"Everyone, gather in the common area. Now." Weegin's voice rang out through some sort of centcom.

First I needed to learn to live with Weegin. He controlled the quality of my life now far more than Switzer ever could. I would win Weegin over. That was a must. I moved to the door in the other room and stood in front of it. It would not disappear.

"Get out of the way," Switzer said as he moved in front of the entry sensor. Nothing happened.

"Great. I bet Freak's fakewire screwed the room up."

Dalton banged on the door. "There must be a computer glitch."

"That's impossible," I said, banging on the door also.

"Use your . . . thing," Theodore said, pointing to his own head.

"What?"

"That's not going to do anything but screw it up more," Switzer argued.

"Can't hurt to try," Theodore said.

"But what do I do?"

"It has to be run by some sort of computer device. The skin must send a signal to tell it which door to open. Do what Theylor told you."

I put my hand over the sensor. Why, I don't know; it just seemed like the thing to do. I closed my eyes and concentrated. Then, on the inside of my forehead, as if someone had mounted an O-dat inside my brain, the streams of computer code flashed before me. The code was jammed by something. I could see it — a little shiny nugget. I thought about what Theylor had told me to do. I got my mind around the blockage and gently nudged it away. At first it wouldn't give, and then it shifted, turned, and flushed through along with the rest of the computer code. The door disappeared.

The other boys just stood there gawking at me. No one said a word as we filed out of our room.

I walked into a long chamber filled with loungers and more O-dats like the ones I had used to uplink my translation codec. The room looked surprisingly comfortable for someone as cheap as Weegin. Everyone was gathered around Weegin and lit by an odd and uneven glow from three arched windows running the length of the far wall. Ketheria was standing by herself and ran up to me the moment she saw me.

"When I ask you to be somewhere, you do it immediately. I don't care what else you're doing," Weegin scolded. "When I say move, you move. When I say sit, you sit. If I have to tell you twice —"

This wasn't how I wanted to start with him. "The door wouldn't open," I said, trying to cut him off.

"I'm deducting half a chit from you for lying, Softwire. It is impossible for the central computer to have a glitch like that without maintenance notifying us," he said.

"But I —"

"Are you questioning me?" Weegin said, refusing to let me explain. "The computer is self-correcting and would detect a problem like that before we even knew it!" The angrier he seemed to get, the more the spikes on his temples twisted up toward the ceiling.

"That's what I said," Switzer shot out. "He wanted us to lie, but I said no."

I couldn't believe what I was hearing.

"Fine, you get his half chit," Weegin said, commending the liar. This was getting worse.

"I swear," I pleaded, trying to start again. "The door was stuck, but I fixed it."

"I will not tolerate swearing, either. As long as you belong to me, you will represent my organization with the utmost professionalism. Children or not, you will behave like adults."

Ketheria put her finger to her mouth to show me not to say anything else. I looked at Weegin standing confidently, chin out and legs apart like he was ready for a fight. But it was no use. I had already lost.

6

When I returned to my sleeper, I felt exhausted. The extraordinary events of the last cycle were draining from my body and I longed for sleep. I slipped the gold disc I'd brought from the *Renaissance* into my locker and put on the plastic pajamas. I avoided Switzer, who gloated over his sudden fortune.

"I wonder what I'll buy with my new money," he said with relish.

"Not much," Theodore said under his breath as he examined his sleeper.

"What did you say?" Dalton jumped to Switzer's defense. "You don't know anything."

"I didn't say anything," Theodore said.

"Keep it that way," Switzer added.

"Leave him alone," I said.

Switzer turned to me. "You're not on the *Renaissance* anymore, Turnbull. Mother's not here to help you."

That was painfully obvious, but I said nothing. He didn't need any more encouragement. I missed the *Renaissance* and I missed Mother, but I wouldn't dare let Switzer know that. I was still determined to give Orbis a chance. I just needed to try harder.

I stood in front of my sleeper. The Keepers had attempted to copy our sleepers from the seed-ship, but the pillow was too small and the bed was too narrow. That was probably Weegin's doing: make it cheaper.

"Don't worry about them. He'll need all the money he has to buy himself a personality," Theodore whispered. "Look, I read about this on the ship."

Theodore tapped the control panel, and the lid withdrew into the wall. Another button released a headset. "This is the best part." Theodore picked up the headset. "You can actually change your dreams with this."

"Change your dreams?" I said.

"Yes. Look at these sensors here. You can adjust for color, sound, and even characters," Theodore said. "If I remember correctly, it's kind of crude. You can select single numbers, groups, or crowds."

I opened my sleeper and cradled the strange headset in my hands. Could it work? I decided to give it a try. I set mine for color: high; sound: soft; and characters: four.

Like the ones on the seed-ship, these sleepers monitored the occupant's vital signs and could seal themselves in case of oxygen loss, severe temperature change, or gravitational variances. I climbed inside, and the cover slid over me automatically.

"Good night, JT," Theodore said.

"Night."

"Night, freak," Switzer said.

Dalton just snickered.

I lay back and closed my eyes. Despite its small

size, the new sleeper was far more comfortable than my old one. I pulled the sheet close to my neck, and the blue light from the sleeper lid began to fade. I wanted sleep to come so badly, but I was concerned about my sister and I couldn't stop thinking about her. Ketheria had spent many rough nights on the *Renaissance,* thrashing about in her pod. I always thought she was having nightmares, but whenever I asked her about them, she acted like she didn't know what I was talking about. On the seed-ship I had instructed Mother to always wake me at the first sign of trouble. It happened often, and I still remember her fits clearly.

"Johnny, your sister needs you," Mother informed me one time, waking me.

I jumped out of my sleeper and raced to the enormous pod chamber where Ketheria, along with most of the younger children on the *Renaissance,* still slept. Many of the silicon nurture pods glowed blue, telling me they were occupied. Only one was rocking.

Kneeling next to my sister's nurture pod, I placed my hand on the chamber.

"How long has she been like this?" I asked Mother.

"She has been in this state for fourteen minutes and twelve seconds . . . thirteen seconds . . . fourteen seconds . . ."

As on so many nights before, I had helplessly watched her through the silicon as she thrashed back and forth, kicking her little feet. Her long auburn hair was soaked. The sweat was dripping onto the nutrition pad.

"Open it, Mother."

"Johnny, waking her is not advisable in this agitated state of —"

"Open it!" I yelled.

The blue light dimmed as the pod lid slid back and around. Ketheria's teeth were chattering.

"She's freezing, Mother." I lifted her in my arms and wrapped her more tightly in the thin blanket. "There's something wrong with her nurture pod."

"The pod is in perfect working order. I noticed a slight supplement deficiency and instructed the nutrition pad to release small amounts of vitamins D, C, and B6 throughout the night. Proper neural stimulation occurred as scheduled. Your sister is simply having a bad dream, and as you have instructed, I have alerted you."

"*Shh,*" I whispered, ignoring Mother and slowly coaxing Ketheria to settle down. "*Shhhh,* Ketheria, everything is all right."

After a while, Ketheria's thrashing stopped. Through it all, she never woke up. I placed her back down in the nurture pod and wiped some of the sweat from her face.

"Please close the lid, Mother."

Now I stared at the lid of my new sleeper, still waiting for sleep to come. I looked across the room: Dalton and Switzer were already snoring. *That was fast,* I thought.

"Theodore?" I whispered, but no one answered. "Theodore?"

Why wasn't I asleep? I was certainly tired. I rolled over, and that's when I heard someone knock on the door.

"Hello?" I tapped the sleeper's controls.

The lid slid back. Everyone was still sound asleep.

Another knock.

"Ketheria?"

I went to the bedroom door. It wouldn't open. My vest! I needed that stupid skin to open the door.

"Hold on, Ketheria," I whispered. I had to get to her.

I put the skin on over my pajamas and went back to the door. It still wouldn't open. I put my hand over the sensor, and just like before, I could see the computer codes blocked — so much for a self-correcting computer. Now the bits of data were fighting with each other. They weren't even trying to get through the glitch. The code pulsed and distorted, shooting streams of green and yellow in every direction. I went to remove the block, but the code swarmed around it.

"Freak, freak, freak," the data chanted, flashing angry childlike faces.

This is computer code, I thought. I reached out and swatted the faces away. I saw the block and flicked that out, too.

The door disappeared.

Instead of the storage foyer, however, I stood in

front of a beautiful bright green forest. The trees were just like the one I had seen earlier on the ring. There were trees as far as I could see. Some with green leaves, some with orange. I even saw a tree with purple leaves. *How did I get here?*

I saw a girl running through the forest in her plastic nightgown. "Ketheria, wait!" I shouted. But she only ran deeper into the forest.

I would not let Ketheria go by herself, so I stepped into the forest and chased after her. The grass felt cool and damp under my feet. I bent down to touch it. Ahead of me I saw huge bushes and yellow rocks. I even saw a six-legged creature with a long bushy tail staring down at me from a tree. The whole scene made me nervous, yet I was intrigued by everything I saw.

"Ketheria, come back!" I shouted. "Look, there's some kind of animal here."

Ketheria, however, would not listen. She ran from tree to tree, trying to touch each one. I followed her, hoping to sneak up on her, when a monstrous shadow drifted across the trees. I looked around but saw nothing. Where was Ketheria going? I needed to find her. I did not want to think what would happen if whatever had made that shadow got to her first. I pushed on, my throat very dry.

In the distance I saw Ketheria stop at a bed of vibrant pink and blue flowers. I almost caught her when she bent down to pick one, but she saw me out of the corner of her eye and bolted.

"Ketheria!" I called after her.

The trees grew taller and taller, and the forest became denser. The deeper I went, the more the forest changed. I saw things I'd never seen in any database: ponds of slimy gold goo, strange gnarled vines that moved out of the way as I approached, and low silver clouds that danced among the trees. The clouds looked like they were playing a game with each other. I also began to sense that more than one . . . thing . . . was watching me.

The shadow passed across the trees again.

What if I couldn't find the way back before I found out what was following us? I stood on a rock to get my bearings. The sky was much bluer now. It was almost glowing, but there was nothing to guide me home. I saw Ketheria go deeper into the forest.

"Ketheria! That's too far!"

I chased after her, but she was moving very fast now — much faster than I knew she could run. And then she was gone. With a jolt, I realized I was now alone. *Where did she go?*

"Ketheria?"

Someone giggled behind me. I whirled around, and in the distance I saw Ketheria sitting on the yellow rock I had just stood on.

"Ketheria?" I moved closer.

Her faced blurred as if she were trying to take on a different shape.

"Ketheria? Why won't you stop? You're making me angry," I scolded her, hoping the tone of my voice would make her stop.

Then, just as if the computer had shut off a light, she was gone. It was as simple as that. I looked around, but there was no sign of her, and I did not know which way was home. The monstrous shadow passed over again, this time on the grass. I looked up. Nothing. I walked over to the yellow rock.

I glanced down and saw the number ten etched into the rock.

10

It looked like a child's initials carved for someone to see. I touched the number. Was every rock numbered? Why would someone number a rock?

Suddenly — *wham!* — something huge slammed to the ground next to me. The monstrous shadow now covered me completely. I looked up and saw a giant flying creature circling over my head. In one clawed foot was an enormous stone like the one that had just missed me. I jumped from the rock and began to run.

Another stone crashed down, just missing me. The ground shook beneath my feet as I bolted away.

I turned to see the vibrant red creature dive straight toward me. Its fiery wings streaked across the green and purple trees. Everything was much more colorful than normal. *This doesn't feel real,* my mind kept telling me. *Where did Ketheria go? Why didn't she stop?* Then the screeching started: the same horrible sound that had rattled my bones when the central computer malfunctioned during our arrival. I tried to look at my hands. As they slowly came into focus, I felt the scorched breath of the fiendish creature on the back of my neck. And that is when I understood.

I was dreaming.

I awoke with a start and bumped my head on the lid of the sleeper. I ripped off the headset and stared at it in my hands.

"Wow."

I looked over at Switzer and Dalton, still snoring. I put the headset next to me and tried to go back to sleep — without it.

The next morning everyone exchanged stories about the dream-enhancement abilities of their new sleepers.

"I was flying," Grace said.

"I was exploring the crystal moons," someone else said.

I didn't tell anyone about my nightmare.

Ketheria came up to me while I was thinking about the number ten carved into the rock.

"Did you have a good sleep?" I asked her. She nodded in reply. "I spent the entire night chasing you around my dreams." Ketheria gave me a strange look. "Tonight I think you should stay in your own dreams."

The common area looked entirely different. It was now filled with tables and chairs. A plate, a glass of water, and a piece of cloth were placed at every seat.

"The room changes with our needs — one room, several purposes. Very efficient," Theodore said admiringly.

"Very Weegin," I replied.

"What's this?" he asked, taking a seat.

On each plate were three tablets.

"That's breakfast, split-screen." Switzer scooped a pink tablet from Theodore's plate. "Mmmm, bacon! Better than Mother's chow synth."

"Hey, that's mine!"

"Oops," Switzer said, and swiped another tablet.

Switzer moved down the row, gobbling up each person's pink pill. By the end of the row, however, Switzer's shenanigans caught up with him. He doubled over, clutching his stomach. As Weegin entered, Switzer straightened and reached for a glass of water.

"Children, be careful with your breakfast. Eat each tablet slowly, with a full drink of water. The tablets expand in your stomach. You will quickly begin to feel very full. The water helps expand the molecules of the tablets."

Everyone gawked at Switzer as he stared back wide-eyed over the top of his water glass. He had eaten twelve pink pills in a matter of seconds and just washed them down with half a glass of water. No one touched his or her breakfast. We wanted to see if Switzer would explode. He put his glass down and laughed.

"This is nothing. I'll eat everyone's breakfast." And with that Switzer gave a loud burp. Ketheria, who stood with Grace between him and Dalton, stared intently at Switzer. After a moment, she took a step backward and then reached for Grace to join her.

Switzer grabbed his stomach and threw up all over Dalton.

"*Eewwww!* That's disgusting," Grace said as Dalton wiped Switzer's vomit from his face.

"Awesome," another boy said.

Dalton was covered in it.

"Quick thinking," I said to Ketheria.

"Yeah, thanks," Grace said.

"Switzer, clean yourself up and then get back here and clean this mess up," Weegin ordered.

Switzer threw up again.

"That's a lot of food for such a little pill," I said.

"And I'm deducting half a chit for this mess," Weegin said. "You" — he pointed at Theodore — "where is your skin?"

"In my room."

"You are to have that skin on at all times. Half a chit." Weegin was on a roll. He went to the front of the room. "The first spoke of each day will be spent in social studies. Here you will be uploading educational and social programs through your neural implants and engaging in social interactions with other ring residents. The sessions are located in the Wisdom, Culture, and Comprehension building on Orbis 1. Travel time: point two five diams. Eat up." Weegin turned to leave. "Oh — I will show you how to travel there today, but only today, so pay attention to how to get there and back. If you're late for work — half a chit."

Switzer threw up one more time.

After a short ride on the spaceway, Weegin ordered all of us into an open-air tram. I wanted to talk to Theodore about my dream, but I never got the chance. I became so engrossed in my first trip to the city that I quickly forgot about the forest and the red bird. As the tram raced along channels cut through the gleaming metropolis, the zillion strange and unfamiliar things I saw quickly clogged my senses. I only hoped social studies would offer me an opportunity to fill in the gaps of my Orbis education.

"What's this city called?" I asked Weegin.

"Nacreo," Weegin replied. "The city of government. All business and dealings for Orbis happen on this ring. Most of them in this city. It's the capital."

The tram came to a rest and Weegin announced, "This is it. The Center for Wisdom, Culture, and Comprehension." If I hadn't known my Guarantor better, I would have thought he sounded a little sarcastic.

Once off the tram, I strained my neck searching for the top of the immense structure. It was larger than any of the surrounding buildings, and the distant starlight made the polished surface glitter against the thinning atmosphere high above the surface of the ring. Within these glass walls, I hoped I might get some answers.

"Let's go enhance my investment," Weegin said, and snickered.

I watched a group of four Keepers move smoothly past us, each clutching a bundle of narrow gold cylinders. Weegin followed them up the steep quartz steps.

"Move it, everyone. Time is money," he hollered over his leathery shoulder.

The inside of the Wisdom, Culture, and Comprehension building was a maze of glass walls and thick beams of colored light that seemed to connect the different levels. The place was filled with aliens, like a spaceway station. We weaved through the crowd, crossing floors adorned with patterns of shimmering stones, and caught the attention of aliens perched on benches carved from blue and magenta crystals. The glass walls curved and bent in every direction, making it easy to lose your bearings.

"JT! Hey, look up!"

I looked up and saw Max three levels away. She was with her group, as were the other children and their Guarantors. She waved at me from the line, and I waved back. Torlee, the Guarantor with all the pink skin and the bubble on his head, was there also. He scowled down upon us and shoved one of the kids back in line. Theodore and I raced toward the spiral stairs to catch up with Boohral's group, despite Weegin's shouting.

When I caught up to Max, she asked, "What's your Guarantor like?"

I shrugged. "I can't complain. Look what he did to Switzer's nose."

Max searched the crowd and giggled when she caught sight of Switzer's swollen snout.

"How about those sleepers?" I asked her. Maybe she could help me understand my dream.

"I know, aren't they great?" she said.

"Any nightmares?"

"I thought that was Ketheria's problem," she teased. "You afraid of your new sleeper?"

"Of course not," I lied. "I was only concerned for Ketheria."

Now I felt silly. I decided not to mention my dream after all. I'd wait and talk to Theodore about it.

"Move along — you're not here to chat," Weegin barked, and pushed me forward.

We all filed into the hollow social studies room. The cylindrical space was eight levels high and encircled a common area located on the bottom floor. Theodore and I entered on the second floor. The humans took up three entire levels. I looked up and watched other aliens fill the remaining floors.

Max walked past me and said, "They're children of Citizens."

"Children?" I caught glimpses of the Orbis emblem, as well as other markings I could not recognize.

"Did you think we were the only ones?" she asked, and stood in front of an O-dat three stations away from me. Every floor was lined with O-dats, each with a neural link.

"I don't know." Actually, I hadn't thought about it much.

"Boohral says the Keepers want us to interact with the other Citizens if we are ever to become Citizens ourselves."

When *we become Citizens*, I said to myself, and watched the many different children attach to their O-dats. I spotted an alien who was a smaller version of Boohral.

"That's Boohral's kid," Max said, catching me staring.

"Boohral has a kid?"

"I think he's more of a clone," Max said, and attached her neural link.

I stared at the alien children and wondered what it would be like to have parents. Even a clone for a father might be nice. I thought I might ask them about it.

"Supervisor. I am Supervisor Keetle," said an alien, growing from the common area on the first floor. There was no other way to describe it. The alien simply emerged from the solid floor, taking shape as he, she, or whatever rose up into the center of the cylindrical classroom. "As supervisor, I will supervise your uplinks and integration of the information into your memory core. You may call me Supervisor Keetle."

"She gonna repeat everything like that?" Theodore whispered from the station next to mine.

Apparently, she was." Information. Anything

you uplink is only information. It is up to you to use this information with practice."

I looked at Theodore, and he covered his mouth so Keetle wouldn't see him laughing.

"Behind you. Located on the wall behind you is your very own link with the central computer. Turn and face the uplink behind you," continued Keetle, never moving from her spot. Her narrow face seemed to look at each of us at the same time.

"She must be some sort of material projection," Max said.

"Gives me the creeps," Theodore said.

"Familiar. Please become familiar with the controls. To become familiar with the controls is your goal today."

I turned toward the display and picked up the hardwire link. *This won't be much use,* I thought.

"Connect. Please connect your neural link, everyone. That is, everyone but the Softwire. The Softwire does not connect. Would the Softwire please show himself?"

Why would Keetle single me out like that? Why did everyone on Orbis have to know I was different? I stayed put.

"Softwire, please move forward," Keetle ordered, and Theodore nudged me to obey.

I slowly moved to the rail. Everyone from the fourth floor and higher wanted to get a look at me. I guess by now my arrival was common knowledge. The news of a human softwire had spread quickly. I felt like one of our science experiments on the

Renaissance — like a bug under glass. I still didn't know what my softwire was good for except opening a few doors.

"Turnbull. Johnny Turnbull, you may access the data files in a manner that is most comfortable to you. Johnny Turnbull, please return to your station."

This was one time I didn't object. I gladly slipped away from the glares of the other students. Max and Theodore were already attached to their neural links. I stood there and stared at the screen. *What do I do now?*

"History. The history of the Rings of Orbis is very important. History will facilitate your existence on Orbis. Please use the history files to practice control. Remember to uplink in small portions only," said the monotonous alien.

A small icon labeled History floated on the right-hand side of my screen. Scrolling up and down the screen was simple; it was uplinking the file that was foreign to me. I practiced what Theylor told me and closed my eyes to visualize the file. It floated in front of me. I could see lines of code that contained the text from the file. Each file was divided into sections. I concentrated on the first link.

"Uplink," I murmured to myself.

Instantly, the stream of code leaped from the file straight toward me. All at once I knew a lot more about the Ancients, the alien civilization that once inhabited the rings. The scholars believed that the Ancients harvested powerful crystals from the moons and distributed their energy throughout the universe. This information instantly became a part of my memory, fitting in with the pieces Mother had taught us on the seed-ship. I now knew that the Ancients used the wormhole to move the crystals to other galaxies, but I still did not know why they left. No one did.

This is easy, I thought. I quickly uplinked another file. I learned that the Ancients built negative-mass generators on each ring to stabilize the wormhole, keeping the "throat" open. I learned that travel between the rings was available by shuttle. I discovered Orbis 1 housed most of the government buildings and main areas of commerce. Orbis 2 contained most of the refineries for harvesting the crystal moons, while Orbis 3 was kept solely for the Citizens' use. There wasn't much description about Orbis 4 except that the defense forces were housed on that ring. *What will we do when we get to Orbis 4?* I wondered.

With all that digested, I still couldn't get the strange dream out of my mind. I turned to Theodore. Now was my chance. "Theodore, what did you dream about last night?" I whispered to him.

But Theodore did not respond. His eyes were glazed over, and he was swaying back and forth, moaning quietly.

"Theodore, you all right?" WhenTheodore did not respond, I moved around the kids next to me and poked Max. "Look at Theodore," I said.

"What's wrong with him?"

"I don't know. Theodore, can you hear me?" I said.

Supervisor Keetle grew taller and now hovered over the three of us.

"Large. The file was too large. This happens all the time. Must uplink in small bits of data when you first start," she said.

Keetle reached out and removed the cable connected to Theodore. He fell to the floor. Two robotic first-aid units wheeled around the rail, scooped Theodore up, then whisked him away.

"Can I go with him?" I asked Keetle. "Will he be all right?"

"Fine, he will be fine. They are always fine with a little rest," Keetle said, then shot up to the fifth level. "Please continue with your studies."

But I didn't want my friend to wake up alone. I thought that maybe if I downed a few large chunks of data, it would knock me out, too. I was gambling that those bots would take me to the same place as Theodore. I uplinked a good-size file, but nothing happened. I tried another. Same thing. No effect. How big was the file he swallowed? I moved over to Theodore's display and grabbed the file he crashed on. Nothing. I found another and quickly assimilated a file five times the size of the one that had knocked Theodore out. I started to think my softwire just might have a few advantages. I decided to see if the computer could reveal any information about the dream-enhancement equipment. Could I link into other people's dreams? Was it the equipment that made my dream feel so real? I scrolled around the screen looking for other icons, something outside Keetle's history lesson. There was nothing. *The files must be stored somewhere,* I thought. I concentrated harder. Suddenly, the wall around my O-dat pulsed bright red and Keetle instantly sprang up behind me.

"Abort! Please abort any unauthorized use. Class data only. Abort!" she shouted at me.

"I'm sorry," I said.

"What did you do, JT?" Max asked.

Everyone was staring at me. I saw Switzer elbow Dalton and say, "He's gonna screw this whole place up if we let him."

"I didn't do anything," I told Max. "I was finished. I was just looking for some more files."

"You're done already?" she asked.

"Back away. Please back away from the display while I execute a reboot," Keetle ordered.

I did as I was told and every screen in the place went dead while the room continued to pulse like a distress beacon. Before the system came back up, the spoke ended and Keetle dismissed everyone. I watched the Citizen children filing out from the upper floors. I thought maybe I could get some information out of them.

I nudged Max and pointed to the Citizens. "Wanna go make some friends?"

"Don't count on it," Max said. "Not many Citizens want more new Citizens. There are only so many resources, and they have a good thing going here. Didn't you uplink the file on the Citizen revolt on Orbis 3? I thought you said you were done."

"I must have missed that one," I said. Max turned away. "Where you going?" I asked.

"Home?" She shrugged.

"That's right."

"I'll see you next cycle, I guess. Bye, Ketheria." She waved at both of us.

The spoke hadn't worked out the way I expected.

I took Ketheria's hand. "Want to hear about my dream?" I asked her.

She nodded and we headed back to Weegin's World.

8

"The first cycle and already two of you are sick," Weegin snapped when we returned home. The leathery alien kicked one of the small cleaning robots. "And my robots are acting up. They shouldn't be acting up.

They're too expensive to act up."

"Maybe you shouldn't do that, then," Dalton said.

Weegin responded in a flurry. His bony shoulders twitched uncontrollably as he screamed at Dalton. "You be quiet! *I'm* not doing anything. Someone is messing with my business. Someone's always messing with my business."

Everyone stood motionless. No one dared to speak to Weegin.

"What are you standing there for? Get to work!"

"But . . . we don't know what to do," I said.

"More waste of my precious time. How do they expect me to turn a profit with useless, underdeveloped humans? Follow me. And keep up!"

We followed Weegin down to the floor of the sorting bay. The humongous robotic cranes continued their choreography as an endless supply of junk waltzed into Weegin's World. Whenever the cranes pulled a container through the outer dome, the protective energy shields would crackle with electricity. In the sorting area, smaller robots sifted through the containers and threw the smallest stuff into large bins that hung in the air.

"Start here." Weegin shouted over the booming noise of the factory floor. He stabbed a large red button on the wall.

The bins began dropping their contents onto the conveyor belts. Up close, I could see that the belts were nothing more than a thin blue mist that suspended the junk just high enough for us to pluck out any scrap Weegin thought valuable.

"The robots can't separate or identify the small stuff. Most of it's garbage that's only good for recycling. Drop it on the floor and the scavengers will grab it. Anything of value drop down here." Weegin pointed to more small bins positioned beneath the conveyor.

"How do we know what's valuable?" Switzer asked.

"Everything you need to know is right here." Weegin held up a neural link. "But go slow. Don't end up like Theodore on the first day or I'll deduct half a chit. Skills first, speed later."

"Weegin?" I asked. "Can't robots do this better?"

"Yes, but humans are cheaper. Now get to work," Weegin said. "And don't get any ideas about finding illegal materials that you can sell in some back alley. The computer has already destroyed anything forbidden."

I helped Ketheria to a stool.

"Not the little human," Weegin said. "She's useless to me. She's too small. I would have gotten rid of her if they had let me."

"What's she supposed to do, then?" I asked.

Weegin rubbed his knobby chin. "Let her do chute runs," he said.

"Chute runs?"

"Lower her down the pipes for any pieces that get stuck, anything holding up the work flow."

Weegin marched to an opening in the wall where the conveyor belts exited. He touched a ring on one of his three fingers. A light shot out from the ring and he pointed it down the chute.

"If you don't clear the belts quick enough, the stuff goes down here and jams it up. Lower the little one down the chute so she can dislodge whatever's stuck."

I thought he was kidding.

"Don't forget to give her a light — they're in your lockers. And use a rope," he added. "I don't want to lose anyone."

"Weegin, you want us to risk her life for this junk?" I said.

"Are you questioning my authority?" Weegin moved directly in front of me. We were almost eye to eye, but the alien was a little taller. "Do you dare to disobey your Guarantor, *Softwire*?" Weegin said with a snarl, and slowly leaned forward. His brown lips curled, exposing a row of sharp, grotesque fangs.

"No, sir," I said.

"Much better," Weegin said, stepping back and placing his stubby-fingered hands on his hips.

Ketheria sat on the stool, and I turned to sort Weegin's trash.

"What are you doing?" Weegin shouted, running up to me again.

Now I was thoroughly confused. "You told us to get to work," I said.

"I paid for useless knudniks," he said, throwing up his hands. "Did you not get any training?"

"Training for what?" I said.

"I should have bought robots," he grumbled under his breath. "You must learn safety. Come here."

Behind the blue misty air belts, Weegin tapped another keypad and a long rack floated out from the wall. He pulled off a sheet of lead rubber attached to a face shield. "Tunics.

Put them on," he said. "Then dunk your arms in here," Weegin continued, opening a hefty trough of gray-green jelly. "Right up past your elbows. Don't worry about the smell; you'll get used to it."

That was a lie.

"This will protect that weak skin of yours from radiation or anything else attached to my valuable property. Nothing gets through that jelly, and I mean nothing."

I put the tunic on and thrust my arms straight into the thick snotty glop. My eyes burned and I almost fell over from the horrific stench.

"Don't be in there very long or the gel will get

too thick," he warned.

When I pulled my arms out, the radiation gel had formed a tough seal around my skin, almost like big rubber gloves, but I could still feel things with my fingertips. It dried as soon as my arms hit the air, but the stench never went away.

"Now you can get to work!"

I started first. I would not let Weegin get inside my head. *Make it work,* I told myself, and I took my place at the conveyor belt.

I tried to imagine that the containers held alien artifacts from some lost civilization or maybe forbidden gadgetry seized from a wormhole pirate. I actually managed to get myself interested. I waited as the sorting bins dropped the junk in front of me. Junk is exactly what it was — so much for mysterious cargo from alien civilizations. The only things I found looked like little bits of plastic, some metal, and a lot of dirt. I kept glancing at the chute to make sure nothing was getting past me, but none of it looked at all interesting, much less valuable. I linked to a sorting file just in case I was missing some rare object.

Before the spoke ended, I found three shoes (I think they were shoes), a laser trigger, and one broken diode crystal —Ketheria actually found that.

And then I saw it. First it was a familiar instruction notice, then a digi of someone I recognized, and finally the doorplate from my own bedroom on the seed-ship. The Trading Council had dismantled the *Renaissance* for parts.

I quickly scanned the computer for verification. I had no idea what to ask for. The central computer was massive. In my mind I began shouting: Renaissance! *Earth! Human seed-ship!* Anything that might tell me what was happening.

Several files containing the name of the seed-ship instantly came rushing forward. I quickly scanned the latest. The seed-ship *was* junked in a deal between the Keepers and the Trading Council. Apparently the human cargo was not enough. The Citizens wanted more. Since he had the Softwire, Weegin got whatever was left over after the others had culled what they wanted. No wonder he was in such a bad mood when we arrived. Knowing Weegin, he would have preferred first pick at the *Renaissance.*

I looked at the other kids. They realized what had happened, too, and were quietly slipping little souvenirs into their pockets. Then it struck me.

"MOTHER!" I yelled.

"What's the matter, Softwire?" Weegin said.

"Nothing, sir. I'm sorry."

"Then get back to work," he ordered.

The disc of my parents' restricted files was no good without access to the main computer on the *Renaissance.* It only mirrored the file paths to the original information, information stored on Mother's system. If they destroyed Mother, the files would be lost to me forever. I searched the central computer for data stored from the seed-ship. I wanted those files.

The central computer on Orbis 1 was completely foreign to me. I didn't even know if I was accessing the central computer or just a network that Weegin used. I also noticed that my translation codec left some things in their original alien languages: weird symbols that I could not recognize.

"That's strange." I made a mental note to figure that out later.

I searched and searched. Then I went over everything again. Many times I came upon restricted files that disappeared in front of me as they approached or changed file names whenever I tried to open them. No matter what I did, I couldn't get around the security codes.

I gave up. I couldn't find anything on the central computer related to my parents' restricted files. I was furious. The only thing that I thought might hold some answers was now gone. They had dismantled the *Renaissance,* right down to the bolts. The ship's computer and its storage devices must have been destroyed.

I looked up to find my conveyor belt nearly overflowing with pieces from the *Renaissance.* Ketheria was plugged in, trying to help, but she couldn't get rid of the stuff fast enough. I dove in and chucked everything onto the floor.

"I didn't want it then and I don't want it now," I said.

By the time we returned to our living quarters, I

felt like an astronaut cut from his lifeline and left to drift through outer space with no hope of returning home. The *Renaissance* was gone. So, too, were my parents' files.

Orbis is what you waited for; it's what you wished for, I tried to reason with myself. But it didn't help. I slumped onto one of the lounging pads in the common room. The room had changed once again. I watched Ketheria fiddle with a few alien games before she headed toward the open doors and the forest outside. But the outside was nothing more than a projection created by the central computer. It extended only a few feet from the common room. Ketheria quickly returned and linked to one of the O-dat displays.

I think the worst part for me was not knowing. I thought I knew everything about my parents: where they were born, what they worked on in the labs, even what they wrote in their notes to each other. To think that there were over three hundred files I would never see made me crazy. Secretly, I hoped to find some *reason* on those files. Some clue as to what this was all about. Why did my parents want to come here? Did they think Ketheria and I would have a better life here than on Earth? If so, why?

The more I thought about it, the angrier I became. My parents should have prepared better for this. Did they know about my softwire ability? Was it possible they knew Ketheria might not talk? My parents performed tests on the embryos for years. Surely, they must have thought of something.

I was mad at them for not telling us. I was mad at them for not preparing us. Worse, I was mad at them for not being here.

When I went to my room that night, I was not keen on using the dream-enhancement capabilities of the sleeper. Theodore was feeling much better by then, but he didn't remember a thing. We said good night, and I placed the equipment far away from me and waited for sleep to come.

The next morning Switzer skipped breakfast. I figured he would skip the pink tablets for quite some time. We found the Wisdom, Culture, and Comprehension building by ourselves and loaded into the social studies class.

"You don't look so good," Max said when she saw me.

"They junked the *Renaissance*."

"I know. Grace told me. But I thought you were glad to get off that . . . tin farm. Isn't that what you called it?" Max said.

"But now there's no way to use the disc you made me to get to my parents' files."

"You're right. I forgot about that, JT. I'm sorry," she said. "I'm sure it was only boring protocol sent back to Earth, anyway."

"Yeah, but it kills me that I'll never know for sure."

"Do you remember when Mother hatched the last of the embryos? When your sister was born and all the other little ones?" she asked me.

"Yeah, why?"

"Remember how crazy it was on the ship? Do you remember how the little ones got into everything and all that crying?"

"I know. I loved it when they would crawl back to the nurture pods," I said.

"And then everything seemed to settle down. Everything sort of found a rhythm. Before we knew it, it was like they had always been there."

"I remember."

"Well, that's what's going to happen here. Everything seems crazy right now, but it's all gonna settle down. We're all gonna find our place, and it's going to be like we always lived here."

I looked at Max. She was smart. "Thanks, Max," I told her. "That helps."

Max smiled. "You're welcome," she said, and linked to her O-dat. "I think we're learning about Keeper decrees today."

Max was so right. Orbis was my home now. Problems or not, this was my life. It was up to me to make it work. I uplinked the files Keetle set aside for us while I tried to forget about my parents' files once and for all.

On the *Renaissance,* Mother taught us about Earth and its customs through the games and having us watch entertainment files. Now we just plugged in, uplinked, and digested the hundreds of rules the Keepers created, all to keep the populace on Orbis under control. Greeplings were not allowed to genetically alter their broods past two hundred offspring (apparently once Greeplings started populating an area, they quickly overtook it, despite their short life cycle). Zzxyx arrivals, as well as anyone arriving through the wormhole from the Theta system, must be quarantined for three phases. All telepaths must report for registration at their first port of arrival or risk being incarcerated, and all Trefaldoorian clones must each be identified by a different name. My new home had a lot of rules, and most of them made no sense to me. I tucked them away neatly in my cortex, said good-bye to Max, and headed off for my work spoke.

Dressed in snotty radiation gel and rubber padding, I stood at the sorting bays and watched as new junk replaced any signs of the *Renaissance*. I recovered an ancient O-dat keyboard, seven platinum screws, and one Khoolan field generator. Weegin rewarded me with half a chit.
This is what they do with a softwire? I thought. So much for all the fuss. On the *Renaissance*, Mother had taught us things like theoretical mathematics, organic chemistry, and even a little about dimensional supergravity. All of that was wasted on Weegin. To him we were nothing more than drones assigned to a task to increase profitability.

During one spoke at the center for Culture, Wisdom, and Comprehension, I attempted to talk to one of the child Citizens. I overheard them on the tram talking about another central-computer malfunction. I hoped to get more details, but the green-eyed alien only called me a knudnik and slid away the moment I opened my mouth.

As phases passed, and one set became three, I settled into my new routine without resistance, but my life felt boring, even pointless. I learned to sidestep Weegin and avoid any penalty from the knobby little worm by dealing quickly with any glitches in the central computer. If the central computer was so great, why did it mess up so many times?

The chits we earned were useless, since there was no place to spend them, and the absence of the contest tank was a big deal for some. Switzer's contempt turned to anger, and I, for one, could not blame him this time. The sleepers became a way of escape, and most kids went to bed early and napped during their rec cycles. I went to bed early, too, but I avoided the dream-enhancement equipment. I only spent my dreams chasing Ketheria when I used it.

One sleep spoke, shortly after the blue lights from the sleepers faded, Theodore tapped on the lid of my sleeper.

"C'mon, Johnny," Theodore whispered.

"What's going on?"

"Birth Day," he said.

I had completely forgotten. And it was even Ketheria's Birth Day. I got out of my sleeper, careful not to wake Switzer or Dalton.

"Should we wake them?" Theodore asked.

I shook my head, and we slipped into the common room. Most of the other children were already there. Grace had managed to steal some food tablets and was filling up glasses with water.

"Happy Birth Day, Ketheria," I said to her. She stood by herself near the makeshift food table. In fact, we all just stood around staring at one another. No one was sure what to do. What was normally one of the happiest days for us on the seed-ship, filled with friends and laughter, was now reduced to a few of us sneaking water and fake-food supplements in the middle of the night.

"It's pretty sad, isn't it?" Theodore said. "I kind of feel bad for her. What a lousy Birth Day."

Ketheria simply stared out the window, emotionless. I couldn't tell if she was upset or not.

"I wanna go back to my sleeper," said one boy.

"Me, too," said another kid.

"Wait — what about presents?" Grace said. "That'll be fun."

"I didn't make one," the kid said. "What's the sense?"

I put my arm around Ketheria. "C'mon, I know it's not much, but it's still Birth —"

An alarm ripped through the common room, cutting me off.

"Let's get out of here!" someone yelled.

"We woke up Weegin."

But I wasn't sure that was it. The entire room was exploding with red and yellow warning lights, just like the social studies class had when I messed with the computer.

I leaned toward Theodore and said, "Something's wrong with the central computer."

"It doesn't matter. I'm not gonna let Weegin find me up," he replied, and bolted out of the room. We found the doors leading to the sleepers already open.

Theodore said, "Something's not right," as he groped around for his plastic pajamas.

"What's going on?" Dalton said, pushing back the lid of his sleeper.

"Shut up and go back to sleep," Switzer grumbled, still trying to sleep.

"Get up," Dalton told him.

Switzer pushed back the lid reluctantly and sat up. He looked around the room and said, "What did you do now, split-screen?"

I ignored him and went into the foyer.

"Where are you going?" Theodore asked, now back in his pajamas.

Switzer jumped off his sleeper and pushed past me. "To see what's going on — what do you think, Malone?"

"I don't think we should do that," Theodore said.

"I want to see what's wrong. C'mon, let's check it out," I told him.

"Well, if you go, I'm not going to stay here by myself," Theodore said, and all four of us, including Dalton, crept out into the factory.

The robots in the sorting bay were going

berserk.

The massive cranes were flinging the giant bins across the room like toy blocks. The containers exploded against the wall, scattering their contents everywhere. Scavenger robots scurried to clean up the mess, but the deranged sorters crushed them in the mayhem.

I rushed to an O-dat and tried to make the cranes stop. I accessed the local computer network, but it was a mess. It seemed like every program in the system was attacking another program. Nothing was in order, and all of the files were either crumbling or had already been destroyed. Only small pieces floated past my mind's eye as I tried to interface with the computer. I frantically searched for something to do.

"COMPUTER, STOP! STOP, COMPUTER!" Weegin screamed, running into the bay. He saw the flying debris and ducked, barely escaping a metal crate.

Weegin dodged the metal monsters while trying unsuccessfully to shut them down. Then there was the noise. A molar-grinding kind of noise. It was the same noise I had heard on the *Renaissance* the day of the docking accident. Even Weegin, who constantly denied the computer's fallibility, would now have to admit something was wrong.

Several other robots scampered back and forth among the fallen cargo, trying to avoid being crushed. Weegin grabbed a skinny robot and heaved him toward the most violent crane.

"Make it stop!" Weegin demanded.

But the robot did not know what to do.

Before it could get out of the way again, one of the cranes scooped it up and threw it out the energy-field portal and into outer space.

Another crane hurled a crate over my head, just missing me. I ducked around a corner and hid from the machine. I may not have liked Weegin's World, but it was still my home and it was being destroyed. *Do something!* I struggled to access the computer from where I hid. I closed my eyes and concentrated as hard as I could.

What happened next surprised even me.

The back of my eyeballs exploded into a ring of brilliant blue light. Instead of seeing the files in my mind's eye, my eyelids melted away and exposed the complex mechanics of the computer. It was as if I had *pushed* my head inside and physically entered the central computer. I felt a rush of electricity across my skin, exploring my face as though something was trying to read me. The horrible noise outside quieted, and soon I was able to see things much more clearly. The colors inside the computer were as bright as in my first nightmare.

Then I saw a small figure, cloaked in radiant green electrons, running through the files. The creature was crushing the files by throwing balls of green fire, which it pulled from its robe. The figure moved like a human, but I could not see its face. Only its eyes pierced the shadow of its hood. *I've seen those eyes before,* I thought.

"Hey, what are you doing?" I yelled.

The evil thing . . . program — whatever — stopped and looked at me. It cocked its head to the side, pausing. Then it ran straight at me, hoisting up two balls of green fire, ready to strike. I disconnected immediately, and everything in the sorting bay stopped at once.

Weegin peered out from under a pile of rubbish. The gigantic room was in shambles. I sat under the terminal, trying to figure out what had just happened. Weegin was glaring at me with an awful scowl. His lips flickered back, exposing his fangs. It would take Weegin a very long time to get everything working again, and it would cost him a fortune.

"I told you I didn't do anything. I swear," I pleaded as Weegin interrogated me in the common room. The other kids stood behind him, against the wall.

"I told you, no swearing. Half a chit."

I rolled my eyes. I told the story over and over again, but Weegin would not believe me.

"I'm not stupid. I knew morale was down, but you did not have to destroy the place. Now you won't be able to work, but I will still have to take care of you. All of you."

"But the computer — there's something —"

"The central computer does not fail, or Orbis 1 would fail!" Weegin screamed. His voice escalated into a high-pitched squeal, and globs of yellowed spit gathered in the corner of his mouth. "We would stop spinning and float off into space, or, worse, get sucked through the wormhole!"

"He is right, Johnny."

"Theylor!" I stood and moved toward Theylor, who had just arrived. "I didn't do anything," I tried to tell him.

"Calm down," Theylor said. "The central computer has record of your sleeper being operated, but not the dream enhancer."

"I don't like that thing," I told him.

"That's not a good enough excuse!" Weegin screamed. "You could have activated the sleeper and then crept out of your room to destroy my sorting bay."

"That will be enough yelling, Joca Krig Weegin. Johnny, the central computer has a record of two people leaving your sleeping quarters prior to the mishap," Theylor said, turning to me.

I paused. "We . . ." I thought about Birth Day. I looked at the others. Grace slowly shook her head.

"See, see!" Weegin was twitching uncontrollably. "He's trying to cover something up."

"I am not!" I turned to Theylor. "There's something wrong with the central computer. There's something inside, but I stopped it," I said.

"Stopped what, Johnny?" Theylor asked.

I looked at Weegin and then at Theylor. They would never believe I saw some sort of program, or a virus, even, running through their precious computer and destroying things at will.

"Nothing," I said. "The sorting bay was already going crazy before we got there. Ask anyone."

Theylor looked at the kids.

"He's done it before, you know," Switzer said.

"What a malf. You're such a liar!" I said.

"Done what?" Weegin demanded. "Let him speak."

"But he's —" I said.

Theylor raised his hand.

"During our first social studies class, he shut down the entire study hall because of something he wasn't supposed to do with the computer," Switzer said.

"Is this true?" Theylor asked.

"Yes, but —"

"And something bad happened to him," Switzer said, pointing to Theodore. "They had to carry him away."

I couldn't believe what I was hearing. Theodore looked at Switzer with astonishment.

"Is this true, Theodore?" Theylor asked.

Theodore didn't know where to look. "Well . . . I mean . . . I was . . . we . . ." He turned to Switzer. "That's not the way it happened!"

"Answer the question!" Weegin screamed.

Theodore looked at me and said, "I think so, Theylor. I was unconscious. I'm sorry, JT."

Weegin almost lifted off the ground. "And you've been lying to me about the doors failing around here!" Weegin yelled. "You're more trouble than you're worth, Softwire." He launched at my throat, dropping his walking stick on the way.

Theylor moved quickly. He raised his right hand, and Weegin froze in midair with his knobby three-fingered hands extended and an expression of pure contempt locked on his face. "I am sorry, Johnny, but this is for your own protection." Theylor turned and waved his left arm over me.

Silence.

I could see Theodore shouting, but I could not hear him. A cloud of milky green fog blurred everything in my path. Ketheria ran toward me, but for some reason she could not get near. Even Switzer looked shocked. When I reached out, the fog felt as hard as rubber. I was floating in some sort of green bubble that hovered just above the ground as Theylor interacted with the O-dat on his wrist.

"Theylor! What's going on?" I pounded my fists on the green bubble.

But no one seemed to hear me. Ketheria grabbed at Theylor's robe as two security drones arrived and pushed me toward the exit.

"Ketheria!" I shouted. "Let me talk to my sister!" I struggled to push the bubble in the opposite direction, but that did nothing.

There was commotion everywhere, and Theylor was trying to calm the children. I was worried about Ketheria now. She would be by herself. Wherever they were taking me, I hoped it wasn't far.

The two security drones guided the bubble

through a maze of corridors and a system of light chutes, before placing it in a sparkling purple stream of light. Everything flashed white for a nanosecond, and then I was somewhere else. Then more security drones attached my bubble to the belly of a spaceway pod. No one spoke to me or even looked at me.

It was the longest ride I ever took on the spaceway. I did not know where I was going, but I hoped it was close enough for my sister to visit me. Though I had already gone so far that that seemed impossible now.

I sat on the floor of my green bubble and watched the stars go by. I thought of Switzer. He had betrayed me so easily. I was just trying to make things work. A large yellow star winked at me from a hundred light-years away. I fell asleep dreaming about what life would be like in that solar system — or any solar system, actually — just anywhere but here.

9

"Johnny? Wake up, Johnny."

I opened my eyes slowly. The green fog was gone. *Where did they take me?* I stretched, examining my new surroundings. My security bubble had been replaced by a large transparent blue box — four walls, one sleeper, one chair, one O-dat, and no pillow. Theylor stood in the corner of the small cell.

"Where am I, Theylor?"

"You are at the Center for Science and Research," he said.

I walked to the edge of my cell and gazed out. I saw a mountain of blue boxes, stacked on top of one another and clinging to the cylindrical walls like chips on a circuit board. A gigantic crystal globe hung from the ceiling, far overhead, bathing everything in a rose-colored glow. I looked up and there was a blue box above me; to my right was another. The blue cell to my left contained an alien that was nothing more than a pin of light floating around the room. Below me was another box. Straight ahead of me, across an empty chasm, was an entire wall of blue boxes. I was surrounded by thousands of these transparent blue cells in a cylindrical enclosure. A giant zoo of unknown species stacked together for what — protection? From whom? I was scared.

"Why am I here, Theylor?" I tapped at the O-dat. Nothing. I tried to access it by pushing in with my mind, but still nothing. Its power was off.

"This is where we will do your testing," he replied.

"I didn't do anything wrong, Theylor. I don't need to be tested."

"I'm going to be your observer," Theylor said. Ignoring my protest, he stepped aside. The back wall of my cell vanished, and Theylor now stood in the larger room that had replaced it. *Where did that come from?*

I walked the length of the new room. It was wider than my cell. That couldn't be right. I checked it again.

"Don't worry, Johnny. This will be your examination room. The effect you are experiencing is called dimensional displacement — a slight illusion," said Theylor, watching what I was doing. "It's difficult to comprehend."

"I'm not stupid, Theylor."

"I am aware of that. I think you are extremely intelligent. Yet the human mind has difficulties comprehending certain things outside its own experience. Consider an Earth painting, for example."

"Sorry, I've never seen a rèal painting," I told him.

"Then think of a digi, a photographic representation of a moment in time."

"All right, a photo of what?"

"Imagine that in this photograph there is a person holding a bucket."

"Okay."

"Can you tell me what is at the bottom of the bucket?" he asked me.

"I don't know — water?"

"Do not guess. Try to look inside that bucket."

"I can't," I said. "A digi consists of only two dimensions."

"Precisely — height and width. No matter how someone holds the digi, or photo, they will never see what is at the bottom of the bucket. And if you lived in that digi, you would have great difficulties comprehending the third dimension of depth because you would never have experienced it. You can only theorize about it."

"What does that have to do with this room?"

"Its size exists to suit our needs. The cell — or room, I should say — next to yours has a similar room that is the exact same size."

"That's impossible."

"It is not impossible if you think outside the digi, Johnny. That is part of what you will learn during our tests," Theylor said.

"Learn?"

"You must learn to break the mind patterns that have dominated human life. These mind patterns have created indescribable suffering on a cosmic scale."

"I don't —"

"Your mind is an exquisite instrument if used wisely. Used wrongly it can be very destructive."

"I'm just a kid. I don't even know what I want

to do when I grow up."

"Johnny Turnbull." Theylor moved toward me and lowered his voice. He directed me to sit with him at the table. "Others on Orbis are . . . afraid of you."

"Afraid of me?"

"You have a very special gift and no one understands why. Softwires are very rare. Human evolution was not expected to see a softwire for another two million years, if at all. I will teach you to awaken your consciousness and become part of a profound transformation happening in the universe. One that no human has yet achieved."

"Why am I a softwire?"

"That is what people want to know, and maybe that is what we will figure out. But . . ."

"What?"

"There is an urgency for our understanding."

"What do you mean?"

"There are those who believe that the malfunctions of the central computer and your arrival on Orbis 1 are not a coincidence."

"I never did anything to the central computer. I mean, once —"

Theylor stopped me. "I believe you, but we must see what you are capable of."

"How long will I be here?" I asked him.

"That is not up to me, Johnny. You will be released when the Keepers and the Trading Council feel safe."

"Safe? That's crazy. I haven't done anything."

"Then your stay here should be a short one."

"What if I don't cooperate?" I asked, getting up. "I didn't do anything. Let them figure out what's wrong with their stupid computer."

"Then your stay will be a long one. It is really up to you."

I lay on my sleeper and stared up at the empty blue cell above me. I hadn't done anything wrong. It wasn't right for them to keep me here. I even caught myself wishing I were back at Weegin's sorting bins. It was hard to believe, but Weegin's World felt like home, and I really missed home. There was only one way to get back there.

"Okay, Theylor, what do I have to do?"

I turned to reenter the examination room, but it had been replaced with the blue wall of my cell.

Theylor was gone.

I spent the rest of the cycle pacing my cell and watching the aliens around me. I spent the next two cycles doing exactly the same. Food was delivered by flying drones that inserted it straight through the cell walls. However, I never felt hungry when the food arrived. Many times the drone returned with more food before I even touched what they had brought earlier.

The aliens on either side of me were not there when I awoke on the fourth cycle. I assumed they were in their examination rooms. I looked out and watched as new aliens arrived in green bubbles and were placed in blue cells on different levels. At first it was interesting to see what kind of alien had arrived, but soon even that became boring. I spent my time pacing my cell and sleeping.

Where is Theylor? I wondered. I stood watching hundreds of flying machines skim the mountain of blue cells and insert a probe into each one. Feeding time again.

"No, thanks," I shouted at the probe as it reached my cell.

But the flying robot poked itself into my cell anyway.

I reached out and grabbed the bot. "Hey," I said, shaking it slightly. "I don't want any."

I shouldn't have done that. Instantly the walls of my cell pulsed a deep red. The robot disintegrated in my hands. My cell slid out from all the others and hovered in the air, high above the open void. I looked down and saw rows of blue cells stretching into infinity. A much larger flying robot shot up toward me. I didn't know what to do.

"I'm sorry! I didn't mean that!"

I know machines don't have emotions, but this one was designed to look angry, and it was equipped with more weapons than I could ever imagine. The machine's massive metal clamps grabbed hold of my cell, and then it injected a whirling probe through the pulsing red wall. The probe methodically searched the cell, stopped on me, and shot a single purple dart straight at my chest. That was the last thing I remembered.

I was back in the forest, chasing the little girl

through the trees and the crystal rocks. This time the number ten was carved into everything. Every tree, every rock — even a small animal scurried past me with the number ten on its back. I did not know why I was chasing the little girl, but she definitely did not want to be caught. As soon as I closed in on her, she would disappear to another spot in the forest. At first I thought the little girl was Ketheria, but she never responded to her name, nor did she stop long enough for me to get a good look at her.

I remembered the large red bird from my nightmares, and I kept one eye focused on the skies.

I knew I was dreaming, so I chose to play along. I wanted to know who she was. As the little girl popped out of my reach once more, I stopped by a tree stump and pretended to find something.

"Wow, look at this," I said out loud. I glanced over my shoulder to see if the little girl had noticed. She sat on a rock but did not respond. I laughed at my fake treasure, but still not a flicker from the little girl. Next, I pretended my discovery was dangerous. I circled the imaginary spot with a grave look on my face. This seemed to work. The little girl strained her neck to see what I had found. I circled around and blocked her view.

Suddenly, I jumped back as if something had snapped at me. The little girl moved slowly toward me.

"Ouch!" I pretended the thing had bitten me. The little girl moved closer still. Soon, she would be close enough for me to grab. I held up my hand in

caution and stared intently at the ground.
"Stay back," I warned her.
She just moved closer. I spun around and grabbed her by the shoulders.
It was definitely not Ketheria.
As soon as I grabbed the little girl, I was thrust onto a scorching desert planet. The ground beneath my feet sizzled, and several birds just like the horrible red one from my dreams flew over my head. Three different suns hung above the planet, and I could feel the heat searing my skin. There was nothing as far as I could see except the birds, circling and waiting. The heat was unimaginable. I could smell my flesh burning. I held up my hands and watched as the skin began to melt off my bones.
    I woke up screaming. A stranger was standing over me.
    "Are you all right, fella?" asked the stranger.
    "Who are you?"
    I looked around my cell. It was blue again. I was lying on my sleeper. The examination room was back, too. I grabbed at my chest where the dart had struck me.
    "Yeah, sorry about that. Security runs on an automated procedure. Don't mess with the mechanics of this place, especially your room."
    "Who are you?"
    "Name's Charlie. Charlie Norton," said the man. He was husky, with flecks of gray hair on the sides of his head. He stuck out his thick hand for me to shake.

I recognized the Earth custom and took his hand. "You're human," I said.

This was a first for me. A human adult. I had never seen one before. He wasn't much different from a kid, only a lot bigger, and he looked kind of tired. His skin was rougher than mine, too, and a little wrinkled around his eyes. Not as bad as Weegin's, but still wrinkled. Would I look like that one day? I was fascinated.

"I am. Chicago, Illinois. Great city: Southport Lanes . . . Wrigley Field — but that got torn down when they outlawed baseball. Illegal genetic enhancements. I still miss it a lot, though," he said, his gaze drifting off.

"Um . . . why don't you go back, then?"

"Time dilation. Everyone I know would be dead, I'm afraid. Different place now," Charlie said.

"I've never met a human adult before," I said.

"And I've never met a softwire before."

"So you know?"

"Absolutely. It's a great gift. The first of our kind. Should make you feel kinda special."

"It doesn't. It put me in here and I didn't do anything. I'm not supposed to be here."

Charlie leaned in close to me and whispered, "No one's ever supposed to be here, kid." Then he directed a wide-eyed nod toward the other aliens in their own blue boxes. It made me smile. I liked Charlie.

"I didn't know there were any other humans on Orbis 1," I said.

"There's a few of us. I was on the second seedship sent out. Quite a while before yours, I imagine, before the invitation from Orbis. I ended up in Centuria. Nasty place. I light-jumped over to Orbis. So did the others."

"There are more?"

"Of course. We all hang out at the Earth News Café. In fact, they made the place in anticipation of your ship. You should come."

"I wish."

"Sure you can. Just do what the Keepers ask and they'll let you out of here," Charlie said.

"Is that why you're here? To get me to cooperate?"

Charlie frowned.

"You're only being nice to me so I'll listen to you. . . ."

"Don't start chewing on your uplink, kid," Charlie said.

"I don't need one. I'm a softwire, remember?"

I stood, turned my back to Charlie, and stared out over the cells.

"Look, kid, I just work here. I heard you were going to stay with us for a bit and I asked the Keepers if I could visit. Sorta makes me a celebrity down at the Earth News Café, all right? Do what you want, but remember that you have a special gift there, son. Maybe you can put it to some good. Help these two-headed monkeys out. Have they ever done anything to hurt you?" Charlie put his big hand on my shoulder. It felt comforting. "Can I come visit again?"

"I can't stop you. You work here, right?" I said, wishing I hadn't.

"Sure, kid. Think about what I said, though. Maybe I'll see you later, then."

Charlie left me standing at the edge of my cell. I felt alone, very alone. I decided to do whatever Theylor wanted.

10

The tests were easy in the beginning. Theylor simply wanted to see what I could do. I showed him how I worked the scanner locks, how I interfaced with the processors on the small robots, how I moved things around on the O-dat displays — all basic tasks.

Theylor then began to hide small programs in the computer, which he told me to search for. It was difficult, and I had problems finding them.

"Your body, the one you use to see and touch, cannot help you. Use only your physical form to connect with your inner self. Feel the life force inside your body, and thereby learn to realize that you are now beyond the physical form when you interface with the central computer," he said.

I understood nothing he said, but I pretended to and nodded. The sooner I did what they wanted, the sooner I could get out of there.

I scanned the computer in my mind's eye and watched the files and programs scoot past me. Some files, though, shifted away when I tried to look at them. The more I concentrated on them, the farther they moved out of view. Theylor's task forced me to go a little farther, so I pushed my mind into the computer. I felt the initial rush of electrons scanning my skin as I pierced the threshold. As I moved around a corner and up a corridor, the dimensions of the computer shifted at my will.

"What did you just do there?" Theylor asked.

I pulled out of the computer and said, "Um . . . I pushed."

"What does that mean?"

"It's like I pushed my head inside the computer. It gives me a clearer look at what I'm searching for if I don't have the name of a file or something and I have to do some digging."

Theylor just stared at me. Both heads tilted in the same direction.

"Does anyone else know you can do this?"

"Why?"

"Do they?"

"Why? What's wrong, Theylor?"

"Do others know you perform this *push* function? That your mind actually enters the hardware?"

"No, I don't think so."

Theylor accessed the O-dat manually and entered some keystrokes while I just sat and watched. He used an unusual language of symbols — some form of Keeper language, I figured. I'd seen it in the computer before, but it was never translated for me. When he finished, his right head turned to me.

"Theylor, why is that so strange?"

"Softwires possess the ability to interact with any computer device by simply interfacing with the machine's controls. As I told you earlier, a softwire uses only its mind to create a cerebral connection. It is as simple as controlling a thought for a softwire, but everything is done within the mind. Somehow, you have managed to put your mind in the computer yet still maintain complete control. I have never seen this before."

"This doesn't mean I'm going to stay here longer, does it?"

Theylor shook his head. "But let us keep that information private for now. Agreed?"

"Sure. Is anything wrong?" I asked.

Theylor's left head stared off into the distance while his right head said, "No. Not yet, anyway." He removed a clear crystal from his robe and inserted it into the O-dat. "How about this?" Theylor said. "Can you tell me what I just put in the computer? I want you to *push* again."

My mind entered the computer. It was getting easy now. If only I had known about this ability on the *Renaissance,* I could have had some fun. I snooped around the computer's local RAM to see what Theylor had installed. Nothing. I saw the portal that led to the network. It was sealed shut. I attempted to pry it open, even will it open, but nothing worked. I looked for little tricks, something different, but I could not find a thing.

What was that?

A flash of green electrons caught the corner of my eye. The program that I had seen trashing Weegin's sorting bay headed straight for the sealed portal and slipped right through. It never paused, not even to open the network or acknowledge me.

What was it doing there? Was this what Theylor implanted for me to find? Was this "thing" something the Keepers had known about all along?

"That's enough, Johnny." I heard Theylor in the distance, but I wanted to go through that portal.

Be careful.

I unlinked from my terminal and sat up straight.

"This was more difficult, am I correct?" Theylor asked.

"Yeah, what was that?"

"It is an advanced encryption seal for data portals. Nothing can penetrate it once it is activated."

"No, I mean the program."

"It is not a program. It is simply a seal, a sort of lock, if you like."

I was puzzled. Theylor was not talking about the program I had just seen slip right through his unbreakable seal.

Theylor stood up.

"Has anyone ever gotten through? Gotten through your seal?" I asked him.

"Never," he said confidently. "It was created with the help of the Space Jumpers."

"Space Jumpers. But I thought they were banished."

"They are," Theylor said, but I swear I saw his right head smiling. "But enough now. You have some visitors."

I turned and saw Ketheria and Max entering the

examination room. Ketheria ran in and threw her arms around me. Theylor observed the hugging with a quizzical look.

"Wow, it's so great to see you guys!" I said.

"It took forever to get here. You must be on the other side of the ring," Max said.

"It only feels that way the closer you get," interjected Theylor. "I will leave you now. I will see you again, Johnny."

Theylor left us to ourselves. I put my arms around Ketheria, and Max, too. I squeezed them tight. I'd been missing them for ages, but they both seemed a little shocked at my display of affection.

"Whoa, you haven't been gone that long," Max said.

"I think three phases would be considered a long time," I replied. "Didn't you miss me? What's been happening at Boohral's?"

"What do you mean? It hasn't been more than a couple of cycles, JT."

Max was puzzled. I was even more puzzled. Even Ketheria seemed confused.

"Max, I've been going crazy, I've been here so long."

"So it's true, then," Max said, nodding.

"What's true?"

"This place, these examination cells — they exist in a different dimension. They've stretched time for you."

"What?"

Ketheria interrupted our exchange by offering

me a strange food I'd never seen before.

"They're called toonbas. They're a delicacy on Boohral's planet," Max said.

"What are they?"

"Don't ask," she said. "Just eat one. They're good, huh?"

"They are, but what's in them?"

"Well, I guess the best way to describe it is a bug. Or at least the excrement of a bug."

"What!" I spat the rest of my toonba onto the ground. Ketheria reached for another.

"Don't worry. They're synthetically made here on Orbis, and they're not from any bug you know. Toonbas are from Trefaldoor and they're a delicacy. Just enjoy them."

I didn't care how good they tasted. Bug crap? No way (but I had to admit, they were good).

"In the real world you've only been gone two cycles. We haven't had a chance to miss you yet," Max said, picking up where we had left off before Ketheria had changed the subject.

"But I've had study sessions, I've gone to sleep a zillion times — I've been here a long time," I said, reaching for another toonba. I sniffed it and put it back. *Bug crap — really.*

"Sorry, it's all temporal distortion to make the — um — prisoners feel like they have been here longer. It's more productive for Orbis. You feel like you've been here a long time, but in reality you don't miss too much work. I checked it all out. Your sleeper back in Weegin's World is still warm, my friend."

"Theylor won't tell me how long I have to stay here."

"I don't think they'll keep you here very long."

"How come?"

"The central computer is still acting weird and you're locked up in here. But they're having a huge tribunal. Everyone will be there."

"Then you know I didn't do anything?"

"Of course, but it doesn't matter what I think. If they find you guilty, JT, you will be banished from Orbis. Forever."

"What?"

Max looked at me. "By yourself. Without us. Without funds. To who knows where."

I looked at Ketheria. I knew I didn't like it here, but I could never leave without her. "I can't let them find me guilty, Max," I said.

"I know," she said, glancing at Ketheria. The dinner drone arrived at my cell, and she moved out of the way.

"Don't worry, it's only delivering food," I told her. "Just don't touch it."

The drone deposited enough food for the three of us, and Ketheria sorted through the different-colored food pills, taking out her favorites.

"Everyone is very nervous. Boohral says the entire existence of Orbis relies on that computer. It was built to never make a mistake. That's why they are afraid of you: you can connect to it and now there's all this trouble...."

"Max — I can actually get into it." She stared at me, and her eyes widened.

"But I don't think I'm the only one."

"What do you mean?"

"When I go into the computer, sometimes I get the feeling I'm not alone."

"I still don't get it."

"It's hard to explain," I said. "It's like I see things sometimes. I don't know what they are, though. Listen, when you go back, I want you to find out if there have ever been other malfunctions with the central computer."

"There haven't; that's why everyone is freaking out. They started when we arrived — when *you* arrived."

"Look harder; look for little things. Like a virus or something," I said, my mind spinning. I could not let them banish me.

"The computer is self-adjusting; it would spit out any virus or any bad code by itself. It's the most advanced computer anyone has ever dreamed of. Don't you get it? If something is wrong, someone else is doing it," she said.

"Then we have to figure out who."

Max and I discussed strategy as Ketheria finished the last of the toonbas, as well as all of her favorite food pills. Before they left, Max agreed to visit every other cycle to keep me up-to-date, and I promised to pry Theylor for as much information as I could. Max said my testing time was the perfect opportunity to dig into the central computer, since it was my only chance to access it.

"I wouldn't let Theylor know what you find, either," Max warned.

"I trust the Keepers. Theylor is a good person."

"It was a Keeper who put you in here, JT."

I had never looked at it that way before.

Charlie did come to see me again, only this time it wasn't for a visit.

"Here," he said, handing me one of the narrow gold tubes I'd seen the Keepers carrying. "This is for you."

"What is it?"

"It's a screen scroll. Read it."

I pulled out the silicon screen, and the notice blinked onto the electronic parchment. It was addressed to me.

Johnny Turnbull:
The Trading Council of Orbis requests your presence at the Center for Impartial Judgment and Fair Dealing on Orbis 1. You must be accompanied by your officially authorized advocate. If you do not possess an officially authorized advocate, one will be provided for you by the Keepers.

I looked up at Charlie. "When am I supposed to go?"

"Right now," he said, and held up a nasty-looking device that was nothing more than a corroded helmet with shoulder padding. A silicon strip with a metallic core dangled from the back of the headgear.

"What's that for?"

"People on the ring are fearful of you, my little friend. Unfortunately this is for their comfort, not yours."

"Do I have to put that on?"

"Afraid so. It's going to make you a little disoriented, but by the time we get to IJFD sector, you'll be used to it. They don't want you messing with the central computer or their tribunal," he added.

"But it's not me."

"Well, let's go prove it, then."

Charlie was right. The protection device made it impossible for me even to see straight. By the time I got used to it, we were already standing outside the Center for Impartial Judgment and Fair Dealing.

"This is where I do most of my work," Charlie said with a little pride.

The perfectly round structure floated several meters above the ring. I could see aliens standing out on the large bladelike platforms protruding from the building, where small craft were also landing. It was the first time I'd seen these fliers. I had just assumed everyone traveled on the spaceway. A large light chute streamed down from the bottom of the sphere. I watched Keepers and Citizens step into the pale purple beam of light and disappear. *That must be the front door,* I decided, and followed a frail-looking alien toward the beam of light.

"One at a time," Charlie said, holding me back. The thin alien glanced at Charlie and then at the apparatus on my head. He quickened his pace and stepped into the chute. I noticed that a lot of aliens were staring at me.

"I look pretty guilty with this contraption on my head," I told Charlie.

"Don't worry about them. We'll get all of this straightened out," he said. "Make sure to step out of the way when you arrive. You don't want to go clogging up the system." Then Charlie gave me a nudge and I stepped into the purple light beam. The effect was instant. There was no time to feel anything. Before I could blink, I found myself inside an enormous lobby abuzz with activity.

The building seemed even larger on the inside. Rows and rows of railings circled the walls. Aliens traveled up even more beams of light to different floors. Small robots carrying screen scrolls flew back and forth between the floors like bees among flowers. Then I remembered what Charlie had told me and stepped off the light beam just as he arrived.

"Follow me," he said.

Charlie walked straight up to the front of a long line and accessed a private O-dat. I saw two or three aliens nod to Charlie as he tapped at the screen. I stood waiting patiently, but my skin itched from the stupid device I was wearing. I forced my fingers under the plastic to get at the itch. The alien next to me left his place in line. I think I was making him nervous. Maybe he was worried that I was trying to take the thing off. I don't know, but I noticed that a lot more aliens were staring or moving erratically, trying to get away from me. I really needed to prove to these Citizens that I was not the one messing with the central computer.

Charlie finished and handed me an ID disc. "Here we go," he said. "Trading Council Tribunal. Room twelve fifty-two. We'll take light chute fifteen-C over there. Better hurry — we're late."

All along the main floor, light chutes carried aliens to different destinations. We located 15C, waited for it to clear, and stepped in. I arrived instantly on the fifteenth floor and stepped off the chute. I didn't have a clue what the C stood for, but room 1252 was straight ahead. The large metal doors disappeared as I held up my ID disc. A security drone greeted me, scanned the ID, and directed Charlie and me inside.

The tribunal was crowded. Aliens jostled for space along the ribbed walls, and every crystal bench was filled. All this commotion because of me. I couldn't believe it. What had I done?

Perched high on the wall to my left was a balcony attached to metal struts that curved up and out from the glass floor. The Keepers sat there. I counted eight, including Drapling and Theylor. On the opposite side sat the Trading Council, or its representatives. Again eight seats, but there were only seven members — four in person and three who had sent their holographs.

The room was filled with a buzzing murmur as more and more aliens tried to enter. But once the crowd saw me, the entire room quieted for a nanosecond and then erupted in a noisy clatter, only now the clatter was focused on me.

"Exile the Softwire," I heard someone shout.

"Death to the human," said another.

"Don't listen to them," Charlie whispered as we took our seats below the Keepers.

With a dramatic flurry, a late member filled the eighth seat on the Trading Council. It was Madame Lee, only this time she arrived in person. Her extensive entourage stood by, almost in an attack position.

My eyes never left Madame Lee. I remembered what she had done to Boohral's assistant when we first came. Her cold stare gave me the shivers.

After she arrived, Drapling stood up and shouted, "If I do not have order, I will have everyone silenced." This quieted the crowd. "You may begin, Theylor," he said.

Theylor rose and addressed the crowd. His image also appeared on giant transparent displays that floated over the center of the round room. "This tribunal has been convened by request of the Trading Council to discuss the rumors —"

"There are no rumors. The Softwire has breached the sanctity of the central computer!" an alien interrupted.

The crowd was on its feet, or whatever other appendages members of the assembly used to stand erect. The turmoil in the room appeared to be more than Drapling could control. Several security drones immediately activated small security bubbles. Pale yellow energy shields surrounded the heads of the loudest aliens, silencing them instantly.

"This is not good for relations between the Keepers and the Citizens," Charlie whispered.

"Why?" I asked.

"There's a pretty shaky balance between those who rule Orbis and those who control its wealth."

"The War of Ten Thousand Rotations?" I asked.

"That ended eons ago."

"They still mistrust each other — a lot."

I couldn't believe I was in the middle of all of this. These aliens were so convinced that the central computer was infallible that they needed someone to blame. It could be anyone, even a thirteen-year-old kid. How would I convince them it wasn't me? Would they believe me if I told them what I saw?

The crowd quieted after Drapling followed through with his threat, and Theylor continued. "Any judgment passed by this tribunal shall be fair and just. All fines or sentences will be carried out immediately, in accordance with the Keepers' decree."

Then, from a door under the Trading Council's balcony, the massive alien Boohral emerged along with his cloned son and several other Trefaldoors. Everyone moved out of their way as these giant creatures crammed the center of the tribunal hall.

"Gaar Boohral," Drapling demanded, "what is the meaning of this interruption?"

Boohral looked around the tribunal. He smiled. His eyes caught Madame Lee's as she stared at what the large yellow alien clutched in his right hand.

"That's a computer drive from the *Renaissance,*" I told Charlie. "What is he doing with that?"

Boohral held the metal box in the air while still staring at Madame Lee. "I have information from the Softwire's ship that will rock the very foundation of this ring!" Boohral's voice resonated throughout the tribunal. Several aliens took attack positions as Boohral's brood circled their leader. Boohral glared at me. "Orbis is in great danger and I can prove it!"

Was he talking about the restricted files on the *Renaissance*? Was he talking about me? What had he found? I wanted to know what was on that drive now more than ever. Pandemonium spread through the tribunal. Security drones bubbled the loudest aliens at will. Theylor hurried quickly down to Charlie.

"Take the boy back — *now!*" he said with his right head, while his left head cautiously watched the crowd.

"No," I said. "I want to know what Boohral found."

"Kill the Softwire!" someone shouted.

"Hurry," Theylor told Charlie.

Charlie grabbed my arm and dragged me through the crowd. I caught a glimmer from the drive still in Boohral's hand. *What has he found?*

"Get back," Charlie shouted to an alien who reached over the barrier and pawed at me. Someone grabbed hold of the device I was wearing and wrenched my head back. I felt Charlie's hand yanked from my arm and the crowd smother me.

"Charlie!" I yelled.

I couldn't see who had me, but Charlie turned around and swung at the culprit. He threw another alien to the side and pulled me to my feet.

"Take this thing off me," I told him.

"There's no time," he said. "We've got to keep going."

Charlie thrust me toward the doors, holding his big arms out in front and ramming his way through the crowd. In all of the commotion, I was still dying to know what Boohral had found on that drive. Was it about me? My parents? It was all I was thinking about when Charlie finally broke through the doors.

The next time I saw Theylor, I felt like I had waited an entire phase. It was little comfort to me that only one cycle had passed in real time. My head was filled with so many questions about the tribunal, it was driving me crazy. I was pacing my blue cell when Theylor finally arrived.

"This time-stretching thing is going to take some getting used to," I told him.

"Let us hope you are not here long enough for that to happen," Theylor said.

"Can I go home, then? What did Boohral show you? Did they find the virus?"

Theylor held his hand up. "Please, Johnny. The tribunal could not continue. Threats have been made against Boohral also. The Keepers have arranged a private session at a secret location with the Trefaldoor the cycle after next. We will know everything then."

"That's it? You don't know anything else? They still think it's me?"

"I understand your frustration. You, too, must remain patient," Theylor said. "As for your involvement, the Keepers are aware that there have been issues with the central computer since you have been placed here for study."

"Then you agree something is wrong with the computer."

"I do not know, and that is why we must continue with our tests," he said.

"More tests! You're kidding me."

"I am sorry, Johnny, but time is of the greatest importance right now. May we begin?"

I was frustrated. Theylor's tests weren't getting me anywhere. And if they were still testing me, that meant someone still thought I had something to do with this mess. I plopped down in front of my display.

"I would like to examine your ability to stay in the computer when you push," he said.

"You mean, how long I can do it for?"

"Yes."

If they weren't going to tell me anything, then I would have to get the information on my own. Theylor's test gave me the perfect opportunity.

"So far you have mastered all of the surface-level user interfaces with the central computer. Now I want to see how deep you can go into the info-structure. I have hidden a file in the computer, called Ketheria, after your sister. I want you to find it."

"Why don't I simply tell the computer to find it for me?"

"The computer doesn't know it is there."

I looked at Theylor. "How can it not know it's there?"

Theylor motioned to the O-dat without answering my question. "Take your time. If you feel anything strange, if you feel too weak, come back to me. Remember to remain grounded to this room."

I pushed into the computer. *If Theylor could put something into the computer that the computer didn't know about, why couldn't someone else do the same thing — someone who wanted the computer to malfunction?*

The familiar architecture whizzed by me as I connected with the computer's user controls to access the file. The computer could not find it, just as Theylor said. Corridor after corridor lined with blocks of data storage stretched as far as I could see. Light encoded into bits sparkled along the corridors — like the trams that buzzed around Orbis. The central computer was a complex and breathtaking metropolis of data. How was I going to find a single file in a computer that controlled a space station the size of a small planet?

I started by sorting any new files tagged with this cycle's date. That limited my search to 345,789,222,505,617,001 files. Not much help. I then accessed all files tagged with any Keeper's personal signature. That helped, but with the entire set of automated tasks the Keepers had in place, it limited my search by only several hundred million files. I would never find this one file, let alone have time to search for information about the tribunal.

But I figured the only way Theylor could get a program into the computer without the computer knowing was to disguise the file as something else — but what or where? Maybe the file wasn't even there anymore. Maybe it had been deleted. I asked the computer for the number of deleted files. That number exceeded my previous search. I asked the computer for the number of files created, then deleted, by Keepers within one diam, during this cycle.

Seventeen.

That was more like it. I accessed the computer for the origins of the deleted files. I needed to examine their origin, so I pushed my way in deeper. If I could simply relink those files to whoever had deleted them, I was certain I would find Theylor's file marked *Ketheria*. Since the computer could not bring deleted files to me, I would eventually have to go to where they were stored.

The computer unfolded before me like an endless maze. Terabytes of info streamed along beads of light to their predetermined destinations, and I was able to shift the dimension of the computer only so far before I would have to push in farther. My body felt like it was stretching behind me, becoming no thicker than a data cable. I turned my head and tried to look at myself, but I only saw more of the computer. I was in Theylor's digi, trying to look inside the bucket. I felt very fragile, and I was nowhere near the location of the file.

But I'm still in the examination room, I told myself.

I made one more push through a cache of open portals to reach the Keepers' storage location: rows and rows of colorful processing cubes, each with more power than a million seed-ship computers, linked together and stacked one on top of the other. The sides of each cube changed constantly as beads of light traveled among the storage devices. I located the spots where the seventeen files had been and asked the computer to link these former locations with files now in the trash so I could identify them. While I still felt strong enough, I retraced my path and headed for the trash.

Every discarded file, unused code, or anything else the computer no longer needed ended up in the trash. There was no organization, and bytes and data were strewn everywhere.

I pushed into the trash archives and immediately stopped.

Standing at one end of a large channel filled with data garbage was the little girl I always saw in my dreams. She was holding the file clearly marked *Ketheria.*

"Hey!" I shouted at her.

The little girl was startled. She threw down the file and ran.

"Wait, don't go. Who are you?"

When I pushed toward her, the little girl fired a stream of dazzling green electrons straight into the channel on the floor. They were just like the ones that had cloaked the mysterious program I had found trashing Weegin's World. Instantly, a pile of trashed data files morphed into a menacing form whose enormous clawed hands thrust toward me. The little girl had used the discarded computer code to create a monster.

The creature's head, with its shining white eyes, rose above the channel in the floor. Its gaping mouth moved closer, as if to swallow me whole. Saliva dripped from fangs protruding from its dark green head. The monster closed on me quickly before I could retreat. A gigantic four-clawed hand whipped around and grasped my face. I screamed as I felt its claws cut into my skin.

Wait, I thought. *If she can create this thing, why can't I uncreate it? I'm still in the examination room,* I reminded myself.

I closed my eyes in the face of the monster, interfaced with the computer, and deleted the trashed files. When I opened my eyes, the monster was already disintegrating. Bytes and pieces were falling off as the rest of the files flushed out through the channel in the floor. The garbage beast's fangs were now reduced to large harmless holes. It was not long before the shape of the monster was barely recognizable and then — nothing. I was in the trash drive alone. The monster, the file, and the little girl were nowhere to be seen.

In the examination room, Theylor waited patiently.

"You were gone a long time. Your vital signs appeared very weak," Theylor said.

I stared at the O-dat for a few moments, taking in what had just happened.

"I . . . if . . ." I looked at Theylor.

"Are you all right? Remember," Theylor warned, "never let your entire essence enter the computer. Always remain grounded to the outside world."

"Why?" I asked, knowing I had stretched my essence very thin.

"Chances are you won't be able to get back out and your body will die."

"You never told me I could die in there." The words tumbled from my mouth.

"I understand some earthlings like to refer to the phenomenon of the soul. If you separate from your body, your soul will be lost in the computer forever," said Theylor, getting up and glancing at the ceiling.

I wanted to tell Theylor about what had happened. "The file was in the trash. I saw it," I told him instead.

"Very good."

"The computer couldn't recognize it because the file had been deleted. If you had accessed it from your terminal, the computer would have known it was there and returned it to you, right?"

"That is right."

"Then, really, the computer did know about it. Is it possible for a file, say a virus, to exist without the central computer knowing about it?"

"It is impossible, Johnny. Everything that happens on Orbis 1 is recorded inside that computer. It is a very, very intelligent machine. Try to comprehend its ability to translate all the different languages instantaneously. If there were something foreign in the central computer, the computer would know about it. It is that simple."

Theylor looked at the ceiling again. In the cell above me, a new arrival slithered across the floor. A snotty trail of brown goo followed the alien wherever it went.

"What's that?" I asked.

Theylor was frowning. "They are known as slopcrawlers," he said, staring at the alien. "Symbiotic creatures. They reside inside other organic life-forms — other hosts."

"Where is *his* host?"

"Slopcrawlers are neither male nor female. They take the identity of their host in most cases."

"Why is it here?"

"I really do not know. I must leave you now, Johnny. Get some rest."

I sensed that Theylor was hiding something from me, but I didn't know what. He was no longer concerned with what was inside the central computer.

"But . . ."

"But what?" Theylor's right head turned to me. It was useless. Theylor would not understand what I had seen. "Nothing," I said.

"Johnny, you would tell me if you found anything unusual in the central computer, correct?"

I remembered Max's warning. "Of course," I lied.

12

I sat in the rounded corner of my cell and watched the slopcrawler spread snotty brown goo all over my ceiling. The creature was methodical. It circled back several times to ensure that every centimeter was covered. I found following the creature's movements relaxing, and just watching it gave me time to think. My life on Orbis was nowhere near what I had hoped for. Especially since the Citizens believed I was a threat to their lives. How would I convince them that something was inside their central computer? I knew I was right. I was absolutely convinced that this virus was causing the malfunctions, but who was going to believe a knudnik, let alone a softwire?

As I waited for someone to visit me, time seemed to stretch endlessly. When the slopcrawler seemed happy with its work, I picked up the slack and anxiously paced my cell. Maybe Theodore would come this time. It didn't matter. Anyone would do, really. Maybe Max had found some new information or something that would help me prove to everyone that it wasn't me, and they would let me out of here. These and a million other ideas raced through my mind as I walked back and forth.

Suddenly, the blue in my transparent cell blinked out for a fraction of a nanosecond.

Did I just see that? I stood very still in the

middle of my cell. Then, for a split second I saw the cell walls disappear, I felt sure of it.

I looked up, but the slopcrawler was circling again and didn't seem to have noticed. I waited for it to happen again. Nothing. *You're going crazy in here,* I told myself.

There it was again!

I could not deny it this time. I was looking directly at the floor when, for a fraction of a fraction of a second, it disappeared — or at least it looked that way. I sat on my sleeper and stared at the floor, waiting for it to change. I was interrupted by the swish of the door opening.

"Max!" I was glad to see her and my sister.

Ketheria walked over to me and stared at the same spot. She looked at me and then took a seat next to me on my sleeper. Max remained in the doorway, her face drained of all color.

"What's wrong?" I asked Max. Ketheria shook her head slowly.

"Boohral's dead," Max said.

"What?"

"He died in his sleeper. They say he was murdered."

"But what —?"

Before I could finish, the entire cell shuddered and dislodged from whatever was holding it up. Max screamed as the cell tilted forward and crashed hard against the cell below it. Ketheria jumped on top of me.

"Hold on!" I shouted as an alarm rang out

somewhere in the building.

The cell shook again, and the wall with the only door to my cell blinked out, revealing curved glass and metal hallways. My cell was only a holograph? It was just an illusion? Within seconds I saw astonished prisoners moving along the hallways, past my open compartment.

My cell tilted forward and shook once more.

"I think we should get out of here. Now," Max said.

"I'm right behind you," I said.

Then, as I moved away from the sleeper, the ceiling gave way, or rather, it simply turned off.

"Watch out!" Max screamed, but it was too late.

The slopcrawler landed squarely on my back, knocking both of us to the floor. I was covered in nasty brown goo.

"What's happening?" said the slopcrawler, its mouth only a slit in its pointed face.

"I don't have a clue," I said, trying to remove the creature's excrement.

"I think we should move away from these cells," the slopcrawler offered.

Max helped Ketheria, and both of them found solid ground in the hallway outside the cell. The slopcrawler struggled to move up the sloping blue box toward the girls, but every time it wriggled, its long body only slid closer to the opposite edge of my cell. I turned to help it, but I slipped on the brown goo and landed hard. Before I could get up, the entire building seemed to shudder. The wall that looked out over the abyss blinked off. I watched an entire blue cell below mine dislodge and plunge into the void. The slopcrawler was about one meter from the exact same fate.

"Stop!" I shouted.

"I'm afraid I can't."

I braced myself against the sleeper and (against my own wishes) tried to grab the slimy creature. My hand plunged into the goo, searching for something to hold on to.

"Hurry, JT!" Max shouted.

Under the slopcrawler's coating of slime was skin like sandpaper. I managed to grab a fin or an arm, and I pulled. The slopcrawler moved a little closer, but not enough. At least it stopped sliding.

In the hallway, Max lay on her belly while Ketheria sat on Max's back. Max stretched forward with everything she had, but I remained just out of reach.

"You've got to get closer!" she yelled. The cell shook again. "Hurry!"

I pushed against the sleeper while Max leaned farther into the cell. Ketheria wrapped her legs around one of Max's and grabbed onto a corner in the opening. We still lingered, fingertips apart.

I repositioned myself, switched hands, and reached for Max. Without hesitation, she grabbed my goo-covered hand, just as the floor holding us up blinked off for the last time.

I watched my sleeper tumble into the darkness as the slopcrawler and I struggled frantically to avoid following it. The only thing that prevented us from falling was Max's grip on my hand. The slopcrawler's goo, however, would not let that last long.

"Pull!" I screamed.

"You're slipping!" she cried.

"You have to!"

The slopcrawler whipped its tail over my head in an attempt to grab the same corner Ketheria gripped, splattering all three of us.

"It's too far," I said, and with that the slopcrawler began to expand, or rather stretch, reaching twice its former length.

"Johnny, you're getting heavier. I can't hold on."

This is it, I thought. This was how I was going to die. I felt Max's hand slip. I tried not to look down, but the slopcrawler's wiggling was loosening my hold.

The slopcrawler tried again. It hit the corner, but its tail slid off.

"Again!" I yelled.

"Hurry," Max said.

The slopcrawler whipped past me one more time. When its tail hit the corner, Ketheria plunged her hand into the slopcrawler's slimy appendage and held it against the wall with everything she could muster. Underneath all that slime, the sandpaper skin held and the slopcrawler began to retract — pulling me up with him. Max got her other hand onto my forearm and helped pull us through the doorway that once led to my cell.

"Thank you," the slopcrawler said.

"Thank *you*!" I replied as Max wiped away some of the slime.

"Sorry about that. A nasty distinction of my species."

"Don't worry about it. Let's keep moving," Max said, looking into the enormous hole over the abyss. Other compartments still fell, some with their occupants trapped inside. We joined the others scrambling through the hallways.

"This is the way we came," said Max as she and Ketheria retraced their steps.

The Center for Science and Research was in chaos. Aliens of all sorts crept, floated, and scampered through the hallways, searching for an exit.

"Don't go that way, Max," the slopcrawler said.

"How do you know my name?" Max asked.

"I was one with your Guarantor, Boohral."

The shock of hearing Boohral's name stopped us short, and we both turned to look at the slopcrawler. Ketheria ran into me and got a faceful of goo.

"What do you mean?" Max asked.

"Slopcrawlers, as you call us, live inside Trefaldoors in a perfectly symbiotic relationship. We breathe for the Trefaldoor. We absorb carbon dioxide while expending oxygen, enabling the Trefaldoor to live in this environment. It has always been a convenient relationship. Once the Trefaldoor matures and develops its own lungs, we are freed, to mature and develop according to our own stages of life. But here on Orbis, adult Trefaldoors still need us to breathe. Boohral's life on Orbis meant imprisonment for me."

"That seems to be a theme on Orbis," I said.

"If you lived inside Boohral, then you must know who killed him," Max said.

"And you know what was on the computer drive he had at the tribunal," I added.

"What drive?" Max asked. "That's not important."

"Yes, it is. You don't know what Boohral did at the tribunal," I told her.

Ketheria was now leading the way as she pushed through the debris and the crowds of stranded aliens.

"And you don't know that Boohral discovered a camp of Neewalkers hiding deep in Orbis 1," the slopcrawler said.

"What's a Neewalker?" I asked, but before he could answer my question, the wall next to us exploded.

"I'm afraid *that's* a Neewalker," said the slopcrawler. "*Run!*"

Stampeding toward us on mechanical stilts were six creatures, half-humanoid and half-machine. Strapped to their oversize arms were all kinds of weapons — cannons, handguns, even swords. One Neewalker fired another shot, and the slopcrawler ducked.

"This way!" Max screamed, and I scooped up Ketheria, never taking my eyes off the monsters.

"Why are they trying to kill us?" I said.

"I think they are only trying to kill me. You are just in the way," said the slopcrawler.

"Great," Max said, and we followed her down the corridor.

The Neewalkers were surprisingly agile atop their mechanical legs. The motorized sound of their legs grew louder as they gained on us. The slopcrawler could move very quickly, but it still lagged behind.

The Neewalkers fired again, and the wall next to me erupted in flames. Another shot hit an escaping alien as it made an unfortunate turn around the corner. Its yellowish skin splattered the wall in front of us. We weaved through the hallways of the Science and Research building as the Neewalkers destroyed everything in sight.

I turned around and stopped at a security panel that controlled a door dividing the hallway. I quickly interfaced with the scanner and the door blinked into place.

"Go, go, *go!*" I yelled.

The door lasted no more than a few seconds. As the Neewalkers tore straight through it, the security alarm screeched frantically. The Neewalkers reloaded on the run and continued blasting at us. Max turned the corner first and stopped.

"Go the other way — this is a dead end!" she cried, but it was too late. The Neewalkers were too close. They had cornered us.

"You should know better," breathed the yellow-eyed Neewalker. His voice was raspy and mechanical, like a bad signal. "You were doomed when your foolish host spoke up." Antennas protruded from its skin through a collar that surrounded its bald white head.

The Neewalker pointed his weapon at the slopcrawler.

"But we didn't say anything," pleaded the slopcrawler.

"Then you should be careful about what you think, slimy one."

I accessed another security panel, looking for something, anything, to use.

Help, I pleaded silently.

Then a blinding flash filled the hallway. In an instant the Neewalker was disarmed.

"Space Jumper!" roared the Neewalker, and the others spun around, ready for combat. For the first time I saw fear on their faces. The air seemed to buckle and a Space Jumper materialized next to me. He was like no one I'd ever seen before: he was huge and equipped like a military machine. With one swoop of his arm, the Space Jumper scooped up all three of us.

"The slopcrawler!" I yelled.

The Space Jumper reached out with his other hand and grabbed the slopcrawler around the neck, and then we were gone. My mind washed away, replaced with flashes of the cosmos, and I lost all sense of balance. But the thing I remember the most, the sensation I could not shake as my body tumbled through time and space, was the overwhelming stench of feet. *Yuck.*

An instant later we tumbled from the Space Jumper's grip and landed in an open field. The Center for Science and Research building was nowhere in sight. I stared in utter amazement at our rescuer while Max, still on the ground, crawled away.

"The slopcrawler!" I said.

All that was left in the Space Jumper's right hand was a fistful of goo.

"I'm sorry," the Space Jumper said. "But you are safe and far from trouble."

His mechanical voice was amplified through a mouthpiece that was attached to his molded helmet. The Space Jumper searched the field using a small telescope attached to his left eye. The other was covered in dark green glass.

"How did you get on Orbis?" Max asked.

"There was a distress call from another Jumper," he replied.

"He wasn't with us," I said.

The Space Jumper looked around again; he seemed anxious. "Follow the curve of the ring toward the crystal moon," he said. "This will get you home." Then the air buckled once more and the Space Jumper was gone.

"Wait!" Max yelled. "Don't leave us here!"

"Wow," was all I could say.

"How will we get home now?"

"Follow the crystal moon," I said, still staring at where the Space Jumper once stood.

"How? There are two of them."

I looked up. It was true; one to the left and one to the right.

"Do you think our hero forgot that fact?" she asked. "Yuck, they were disgusting."

"Who, the Neewalkers or the Space Jumper?"

"Both," she said.

Ketheria tugged on my sleeve and pointed at the moon to the right. She started walking in that direction. I looked at Max and shrugged. *We have to get home.* I followed Ketheria. Max glanced up at the moon on the left, shrugged, and fell into step behind us.

13

The three of us walked in silence toward a forest of trees and enormous crystal rocks. We kept the moon in front of us, just like the Space Jumper said to. The ring's horizon reappeared over the top of the forest, curving up and disappearing into the thin clouds. There was no sign of home.

"I wish I had had more time to talk to the slopcrawler, you know, about the drive," I said, breaking the silence.

"What would a computer drive from Earth have to do with Orbis?"

"My point exactly!"

"No. Boohral was always complaining about the Keepers. About how he mistrusted them and how he was convinced they were trying to take back control of Orbis."

"But they have nothing to gain," I said. "If anyone is sabotaging the computer to get some sort of control, it can only be the Trading Council."

"Why? Their businesses depend on it. That seems kind of dumb, don't you think?"

"I don't know," I told her. "The way Theylor made me work the computer — it felt like he was using me to figure something out."

"But what?"

I stopped and turned to my friend. "There's something in the computer, Max. Someone put something in the computer, and the Keepers are trying to find it."

Max rolled her eyes and shook her head once more. "Not this again. If there was something in the computer, the computer would know and spit it out. It's that simple."

"I can get in there. How come it doesn't spit me out?"

Max shrugged. She didn't have an answer.

"I wish you would believe me, Max."

"It really doesn't matter what I think. If the slopcrawler was right and there is an army of Neewalkers somewhere on the ring, it can only mean that they're getting ready for a war."

"Well, I didn't fly halfway across the galaxy just to get blown up," I told her. "Don't you wonder if there isn't more? Something bigger, something better?"

"No. I'm thirteen."

"If this *is* it, if our parents were just fooled into working for these aliens, then I'll help Switzer steal the first starship he can find and we're out of here."

"Don't tell him that. He'll hold you to it."

I stopped when I reached the edge of the forest. Ketheria was already several steps beyond the tree line before I noticed it.

"What's the matter now, JT?" Max asked.

"I've been here before."

"Yeah, right." Max grabbed me by the arm, but I pulled away.

"In my dreams. I once thought I was chasing

Ketheria through this forest, but it wasn't her. I think it was the thing I found inside the central computer."

Ketheria cautiously stepped out of the forest.

"A dream? Now you're telling me the thing you think is screwing up the central computer is also in your dreams? C'mon, I'm hungry," Max said, moving into the forest without us. Ketheria waited for me and we walked in together.

The forest unfolded precisely as in my dream. I looked up to see if that horrible red bird still circled the treetops. Ketheria followed my gaze as if she knew exactly what I feared. I stopped at a large boulder whose shell was cracked, letting the purple crystal core shine through. The last time I saw this rock, the number ten was carved into the top of it. Ketheria ran her hand over the spot I was staring at.

Unlike in my dream, however, Ketheria stayed by my side and the winged red creature never arrived.

"Don't worry, Ketheria. Max is right: it was just a dream."

I heard the sound of rushing water. It grew louder as we walked through the forest.

"Is there water near Weegin's World?" Max asked.

"Not that I know of."

Were we going the right way?

When we cleared the forest, the sound of rushing water became deafening. We stood at the edge of a deep pool that spilled toward a majestic palace cut into the side of a giant waterfall. Smaller rises around the palace created more waterfalls, some of which even passed right through the walls. I could not see where the water was coming from or where it was going. It was as if the water was only used for decoration. Lush plant life was everywhere, and several of the red birds that I once feared now soared over the water looking far less dangerous than before, almost beautiful.

"That doesn't look like home to me," Max said.

"Who do you think lives here?" I wondered aloud.

"I have no idea."

As I looked closer, I noticed that the palace was more like a small city. I looked down and saw several marbled stones rise in front of us and hover just above a pool of crystal clear water, as if beckoning us forward. Ketheria stepped onto the first one.

"Wait, Ketheria. This is not the way home," I said, and another stone appeared. Soon there was an entire path that guided us to the unknown city.

"I'm following her," Max said.

"Fine."

With Ketheria in the lead, we stepped carefully across the stones and through the mist rising from the water cascading all around us.

"Keepers," Max said, pointing to the two-headed creatures scurrying around above.

"Is this where they live?" I said, as I stepped off the last of the stones and onto a broad stairway that rose up and into the city.

"I don't know, but they're in an awful hurry."

When we reached the city, we strolled through the streets undisturbed as Keepers rushed by us, hardly noticing we were there. Fresh fruit hung from vines, and every stone, every piece of metal, was carved in intricate patterns and symbols. And water was everywhere. It rushed through channels and spilled into pools. In some places, the water rushed upward, as if it was immune to gravity.

Max attempted to stop a Keeper by reaching for his purple robe, but all he did was stare at her with one head while charging forward, guided by the other.

"Something's wrong," I said. "I can feel it."

"They must know the Neewalkers attacked the Science and Research building," Max said, and Ketheria nodded in agreement. Then Ketheria reached up and plucked a thick, fleshy fruit from a tree.

"Be careful, Ketheria — you don't know what that is," I warned her.

Max took the fruit from Ketheria and sniffed it.

"Smells sweet." She bit into it as Ketheria tried to take it back. "Softer than an apple . . . it's really good, JT." Max held it up for me as the juice ran down her chin. I declined and Ketheria snatched it away. "Careful. It's hard in the middle," Max added.

I saw a Keeper pass through a small archway at the end of a cobbled lane.

"We need to ask one of these guys how to get home," I said, and I followed him. We turned the corner, and the alien descended a flight of stairs that appeared to go under the building.

"That's not the way home, either," Max said, staring down the darkened flight of stairs.

"C'mon, someone down here should be able to tell us how to get back."

The stairwell was damp, and the fresh, earthy smell of mold was strong. The stone steps led so far down I couldn't see the end of them. *If Theodore were here, he would be counting the number of steps right now. Maybe I should, too*, I thought.

The stairs reached a series of cavernous rooms with rows of odd, identically shaped pillars. This place was nothing like the surface. Small circular craft, each navigated by a single Keeper, hovered across the pillar tops. The only light, a cool greenish glow that cast creepy shadows on the metal-plated walls, came from these vehicles.

Max peeked down the rows of pillars, watching the green glow as the vehicles descended deeper into the underground. She rubbed her forehead. "I would love to look inside one of those machines, but I'm not too crazy about this, JT," she said.

"Don't worry," I reassured her. "I'm sure Theylor is here somewhere."

She looked around the enormous cave. "But it's impossible for a room this size to exist under the building we just entered," she said.

"Dimensional displacement," I replied.

"What?"

"Pretend you live in a digi and you're holding a bucket. . . ." I started to explain Theylor's lesson but hesitated after seeing the incredulous look on Max's face. "Forget it. C'mon."

The path of pillars opened onto an oval room filled with a soft golden glow. Several of the craft hovered, as if waiting. The air was thick, sweetened by a tangy smell, and the room was deathly quiet. I could even hear myself breathing. I moved off the path and away from the pillars.

"This way," I told the girls, and stopped on a balcony high above a crowd of Keepers, who were circling a pool of slick black water. I could see symbols flickering from lights hidden deep in the pool.

"There's Drapling," Max said.

"*Shhhh.*" I sensed we would not be welcome. "Don't even breathe." I worried someone would find us before we found Theylor.

Drapling stood at the top of the pool on an ornate riser carved from the same stone that decorated the city. I peered down on the ceremony. Drapling raised his arms above his heads and spoke loudly.

"Reality is the result of our thoughts!"

"*So say the Descendants of Light,*" chanted the other Keepers.

"The Ancients are the Original Architects!"

"*So say the Descendants of Light.*"

Every time the Keepers responded, strange

symbols formed inside the pool of black water: the same symbols Theylor had used when he accessed my O-dat during my stay at the Science and Research building. Each time Drapling spoke, the secret writings swirled away and were replaced by a new set of symbols.

"Only when we believe things are possible will our reality change!"

"So say the Descendants of Light."

Drapling lowered his hands, and seats rose from the ground around the pool of black water.

Max whispered, "I think we should get out of here, JT. I don't see Theylor, and I don't like that Drapling guy."

I held up my index finger. I wanted to see what they were talking about. I wanted to know what those symbols meant.

"We were incarnated on this ring to labor for the Ancients," Drapling preached from his stone. "To harvest the life-giving crystal from Brother and Sister moon and, through the great wormhole, spread this quintessence throughout the universe." Drapling paused and leaned forward. "While we wait, powerless, for a sign from the Ancients, our duty to them has been defiled. Those among us who strip our Brother and Sister for profit have infected the Supreme Intelligence. They wield their power not to spread the message of the Ancients but for their own personal gain. We have begun to serve them more than we serve the Ancients!"

Drapling stood tall. The other Keepers could not

sit still, and their pale blue skin flushed red with anger.

"Friends, Descendants of Light, now is the time. The enemy will soon attack. It is our responsibility to cleanse Orbis and revive the true intentions of the Ancients!"

The Keepers let out a screech that rocked the very footing we stood on. Ketheria dropped the large fruit pit that she still clutched in her hand. I watched in horror as the fruit seed rolled over the edge and tumbled toward the Keepers.

"Let's get out of here," Max breathed, but before we could move, the pit splashed into the pool of water. Their screeching halted as the Keepers stared at the ripples on the pond in disbelief. Drapling's heads shot up toward us, but we didn't hang around to find out if he had seen us.

"Find them!" I heard Drapling shout.

We scurried back into the shadows along the walls and crossed the oval room.

"Why are they chasing us?" Max asked.

"I'm not sticking around to find out."

I grabbed Ketheria's hand while Max followed. The room ended with a large maze of walkways over a pitch-black void.

Ketheria stopped in her tracks. She did not want to cross.

"We have to, Ketheria," I urged her. Ketheria shook her head stubbornly.

"I'm with her on this one," Max whispered.

The screeching from the Keepers grew closer.

"We can't go back," I said, and pulled Max and Ketheria onto the walkway.

I did not look down, but it was so dark that I don't know if I would have seen anything, anyway. *Just keep moving,* I told myself, but the farther I got, the thicker the air became. I found it increasingly hard to breathe. I looked behind me, and I could hear Keepers where we once stood but couldn't see anything. The Keepers now sounded kilometers away.

It became harder and harder to lift my legs. Ketheria's hand felt too heavy for me to hold, and it slipped from my grip. At that moment I wondered if our capture would have been a better outcome.

"Ketheria," I breathed, but the word barely made it out of my mouth. I could not lose her here.

I slowed to a crawl. It felt like a giant gravity cushion from the spaceway was pushing down on my entire body. I tried to call out for Max, but the pressure on my lungs left the words on my lips. Falling down seemed as hard as standing up. After a few more steps, I couldn't breathe, let alone go back. A small light blinked in front of me, then I blacked out.

14

I opened my eyes and the next thing I saw was the lid to my sleeper at Weegin's World. I pushed the lid back and sat up. Switzer was snoring, as usual, and Dalton was asleep below him. My head was pounding.

"Where did you go?" Theodore was awake.

"Where is Ketheria? Is Max back, too?" I whispered to Theodore, getting off my sleeper.

"I don't know. They brought you back a while ago." Theodore rubbed his eyes and I went for the door.

"Who brought me here?"

"Security drones. Where are you going?"

"I want to see if Max and Ketheria are all right."

"Max?" he said. "JT, Max is not here."

I tapped into the door scan to get my vest.

"JT," Theodore said, pointing to his implant port, "just search the security controls to see if Ketheria's in her sleeper."

"You're right." I did just that and slipped into the local network from the door scan. I accessed security, and there was Ketheria. I assumed Max made it home, too.

"Where have you been all this time? Weegin said you were in prison."

"Why didn't you come to see me?" I asked him.

"Weegin wouldn't let me."

"But Ketheria came," I said.

"I guess because you're her brother. He really didn't seem to care what she did," Theodore said. "JT, aren't you going to tell me what happened?"

But I didn't know where to start. Instead I said, "What's been happening here?"

Theodore whispered anxiously. "There's talk of war. Weegin has doubled the work shifts to repair his factory. He says the Keepers are trying to destroy his business. He said you work for the Keepers."

"I don't work for anyone. The Keepers and the Citizens have it all wrong. There's something *in* the central computer that's doing all of this, but they can't see that."

"How do you know?" Theodore asked.

How did I get home? Who brought me here?

"JT?"

I looked at Theodore. "I saw it," I said.

"I saw the virus inside the central computer. It looks like a little girl." My head hurt. "Let's go back to sleep," I said.

"But..."

"I'll tell you in the morning. Everything. I need to sleep," I said, quickly getting back into my sleeper. I didn't want to talk and I was deathly tired. Besides, I couldn't explain it even if I wanted to.

Things seemed different at Weegin's World now. Switzer was ostracized for snitching on me. Weegin avoided me at every turn and didn't say a thing about the Science and Research building or why I was back. But none of that measured up to the moment Max walked through the main door.

All the children from Boohral's group had been dispersed among the remaining Guarantors. Max arrived home to find a screen scroll that told her to report to Weegin's immediately. It seems Boohral did not make proper arrangements for the placement of the children before his death, so they could not be willed to Boohral's brood. This was one Keepers' decree that I certainly agreed with. Where she could have ended up was any alien's guess.

Weegin, however, now complained that there were three more mouths to feed.

When Max and the others joined everyone in the common room, they bombarded her with questions.

"What was your place like?" someone asked.

"Was it better than here?" said another child.

Max looked around. "No. Maybe a little bigger." She noticed the garden and pointed. "Wow! Ours only opened onto the Trading Hall."

"You've been to a trading chamber?" Theodore asked.

"Yeah. You don't have to stay here during your recreation period, you know. Didn't Weegin tell you?"

Weegin made busy in the corner as if he had never heard Max.

"And he's supposed to credit your account with

the proper amount of chits every four cycles. Isn't that right, Weegin?" Max said, aware that he was avoiding the discussion by tending to his larva.

"We can leave here? Anytime we want?" Switzer shouted.

"Weegin?" Max pushed the subject.

"Yes," Weegin said sheepishly.

Almost every child bolted for the door.

"How do we access our chits?" Dalton asked.

"Just give them your name and they'll scan your vest," Max said. "By the way, Weegin, I'll be needing a new skin."

"It will be sent shortly . . . pesty one. No one deserves anything, you know. Not with the state my business is in. You're lucky they don't ship you through the wormhole."

I was too happy to care about Weegin's empty threats.

Ketheria and I followed Max to the Trading Hall. Theodore was just as excited as I was and he joined us, too. During the trip on the spaceway, I told him about what happened to me at the Science and Research building, and Max told him about Boohral's death. But our conversation quickly turned to the use of money and all the things we had read about life on Earth when we were on the *Renaissance.* I was anxious to see the stores and shopkeepers. I had no idea what to expect, but the chambers in the Trading Hall provided everything I ever dreamed of and more.

Strange, exotic items from all over the galaxy were on display. I saw speaking animals from the Theta system, metallic fabrics spun from the worms of Gia right before my eyes, and the most amazing alien gadgets. Ketheria purchased some small rubber balls called glowglobes. When she dropped one, it would light up and slide across the ground or bounce in some direction that defied all laws of physics. Ketheria chased them endlessly around the Trading Hall.
    I breathed in the intoxicating aromas of alien food cooked out in the open, and the girls purchased a couple of pouches of toonbas to munch on. Theodore enjoyed them much more than the food pills we ate, even after I told them what they were made of.
    "I like this," I told Theodore as we walked through the trading chambers.
    "Look," Max said, pointing to several aliens shuffling by dressed in red and white silk robes. Their faces were painted white, with colored spiral markings, and their feet were bound tightly together. The aliens walked very slowly, with their arms extended to the side. "They're studying to be Nagools."
    "What's that?" Theodore asked.
    "They study OIO. Boohral took it very seriously. It's from the Ancients. It's the art and science of cosmic energies," Max said, shrugging.
    It was like that everywhere I turned. I could have stayed at the Trading Hall for a whole rotation

and I would have seen something new on every corner. I loved it. All my worries about the central computer were quickly slipping away, and I was happy.

Then I saw Switzer. He was bragging to Dalton and another kid when Max strolled up to him.

"Only two chits and it can open any door I want," Switzer said, as he held up the crystal, admiring it. "No need to wear this stupid skin anymore."

"You'll get caught," Theodore warned him.

Switzer turned to see us standing there. "If you say anything, split-screen, I'll clobber you," he threatened. "You, too, *Dumbwire*."

Max pulled open Switzer's vest, then showed him the crystal in her own.

"He swiped your own crystal, you idiot, and sold it back to you. He probably scanned it and saw you couldn't afford much more than two chits," she said.

Switzer felt his vest and then grabbed Dalton and checked his. Max was right. There was no crystal in his skin.

"It happened to someone at Boohral's," she said to me. "It's only programmed to open doors you are authorized for, anyway. Did you even try a door you've never been able to access before?" Max asked Switzer.

"You bought your own crystal sensor?" Theodore laughed.

Switzer took a step toward Max. He didn't like

to be made fun of by a girl.

"If you weren't a girl, I would . . ."

"What? I'm not afraid of you," Max said.

I moved to get between them. "Back off, Switzer."

"You're lucky your boyfriend is here."

"He's not my boyfriend," Max said.

Switzer took a step back, smiling. "It's pretty convenient, isn't it?" he said.

"What is?" I asked.

"Boohral kept your little girlfriend away and now he's dead. I'm sure they're going to be asking a lot of questions, probably another tribunal. Maybe I should let them know I have a few things to say. Take you away again."

"Go away, Switzer," I told him. I was finished with his constant conspiracies. He was only sore because he had just wasted two chits on something he already owned and Max had proved it in front of everyone.

"C'mon, guys," I said, and led everyone away from Switzer. "Ketheria, show us where you got those toonbas."

"That guy is such a malf," Theodore said when he knew he was far enough away that Switzer couldn't hear.

"He might be right, though," Max said.

"What? You don't think I had something to do with Boohral dying?"

"Of course not. I'm just saying, some people might say something. Boohral died from a malfunction of his sleeper. The central computer controlled his sleeper. They like pointing their fingers at each other around here, haven't you noticed?"

"Well, I don't think there's enough of Science and Research left to lock me up there again," I said, but all my worries came rushing back. How was I going to convince anyone that something was inside their precious computer? It wouldn't be long before another Citizen pointed a finger at me again. The thought of it made me angry. I had done nothing wrong. And I would not let them lock me up again.

That's when Ketheria grabbed my vest and pulled me back.

Several Neewalkers had cornered a group of the dusty dirt aliens, the same kind that Max ran into when we first arrived.

"I was standing there!" yelled the little creature, which resembled a grimy accordion. "Rarely am I aboveground, and you must stand there also?"

The Neewalkers laughed and moved their stilts wherever the dirt aliens moved. It only infuriated the dusty creatures more, but that was the goal of the Neewalkers.

"Now you want to be here! Extremely irregular!"

I walked straight toward the Neewalkers. Ketheria tried to stop me, but I got their attention anyway.

"Hey, leave them alone!" I shouted.

The tallest Neewalker turned toward me and

drew a sword so fast it looked like it came out of his skin. Every other Neewalker followed his lead. I had succeeded in taking attention away from the dirt-covered aliens, but now every Neewalker was pointing his weapon at me.

"Why are you bothering them?" I demanded. "I'm sure the Trading Council has better things for you to do, like hunting down slopcrawlers."

"We know of no mission," breathed the Neewalker. The red markings on his ghastly face twitched, telling me he was lying. He scraped his sword along my chin. "But we are looking for one."

"Leave him alone," Max said.

"Feisty, for such weak creatures," the Neewalker said. "I like it. What do you want for this one?" He inched toward Ketheria. His metal stilts blinked and whirled as he moved.

"She's not for trade!" I said.

Computer chip.

I scanned the Neewalker as he reached for Ketheria. There it was, plain as day — the Neewalker's stilts were run by a computer attached to its brain. I pushed into the chip and grabbed the first thing I could find.

The Neewalker's right stilt gave out just before he touched Ketheria, and he crashed to the ground. His red-and-white face was awash in shock. He wheezed and whirled, trying to get control of his leg. For a split second I wondered if the little girl inside the central computer felt this way whenever she manipulated something on Orbis.

A large Neewalker reached out and grabbed me by the collar, lifting me into the air.

"The Softwire," he said.

"It should be worth something," the fallen Neewalker said.

"Take Ketheria," I ordered Theodore, but Max was already one step ahead of me. The three of them ran for help while the Neewalkers looked me over as if they had found a crystal on the ground. I pushed into the next Neewalker.

One more Neewalker arrived, but I recognized this one. It was the yellow-eyed one from the Science and Research building. "Let him be, Chiu Layn," he ordered.

"But Sar Cyrillus, this is the Softwire," he said.

"Yes, I know. We do meet under the most unusual circumstances, don't we, Softwire?" Sar Cyrillus said in a raspy tone. "You've become quite a pain." He looked down at his crippled comrade.

I struggled to free myself from Chiu Layn's grip, but it was useless.

"I did not know he was the Softwire," said the red-and-white-faced alien, still trying to get up.

"This is a perfect demonstration of the fact that you must assess your enemy before engaging. Otherwise, what good are you?" Sar Cyrillus said.

Sar Cyrillus raised his hand and waved it over the collar of the downed Neewalker. The effect was death; the Neewalker fell still.

"Do you see how easy it is?" Sar Cyrillus said, turning his attention back to me. "I could be rid of you as easily" — Sar Cyrillus examined his hand with admiration — "but some believe you are useful, and I'm paid to do what I'm told," he said, dropping his hand with feigned disappointment.

"What's going on here?" someone behind me said.

I turned. "Charlie!" I shouted.

"It doesn't look like your friends here are playing fair, Johnny." Charlie drew a slick silver weapon that snuggled neatly in his big hand. The Neewalkers took a cautious step backward as my friends returned with eight security drones. The sight of the security drones only made the Neewalkers laugh, but they never took their eyes off the weapon in Charlie's hand. Chiu Layn dropped me, and the other Neewalkers collected the dead one.

"We *will* finish this," Sar Cyrillus snarled.

The security drones followed the Neewalkers as they walked away.

"Are you all right, buddy?" Charlie asked.

"Yeah, thanks, Charlie. Good work getting the drones," I said to Max.

"Ketheria found them, but I think the Neewalkers were more afraid of that," Max said, pointing to Charlie's gun.

"This? You kids shouldn't be seeing that." Charlie tucked the weapon out of sight. "My name's Charlie. You must be Max and Theodore. And you must be Ketheria," he said, bending down to her eye level. She moved behind me. Ketheria had never seen a human adult before.

"She's a little shy," Max said.

"She certainly looked ready to take on those Neewalkers. C'mon, let me get you kids something to eat. You must be hungry."

Ketheria wasn't shy anymore once the big man mentioned food. She took my hand and we followed Charlie through the Trading Hall.

Charlie took us to the Earth News Café. It was a shrine to everything earthly. Plasma screens showed digis of Earth cities and holographs of famous digital stars, and they even played music from Earth.

"When did they make this place?" Max asked.

"They did it when they knew your parents were coming," he replied. "Makes ya miss home, doesn't it, kids?"

"Not really," I told him, looking for something familiar in the pictures on the café walls. I thought of my parents and their lives on Earth, but Earth felt as foreign as any other planet I'd ever read about. Even though I was nothing more than a slave on Orbis, it still felt more like home to me than Earth.

"That's right. You've never been to Earth. Very crowded planet. Always cloudy now, too."

Charlie led us to a table, where he introduced each of us to his friends.

"Everyone, this is Johnny Turnbull, the softwire I told you about. These are his friends Max and Theodore and his sister, Ketheria," he said.

"Pleased to meet you. I'm Albert," said a very

tall human with messy hair and thick glasses. Albert knocked over his drink as he got up.

"Ah, Albert, now look what you've done." A short plump woman with pretty eyes scolded him. "I'm Rose. It's a pleasure to meet you. It's so nice to finally have some more humans on Orbis. We thought Charlie was pulling our leg when he said he'd met the Softwire. And you're one of ours, for that matter."

"C'mon, kids, sit down," Charlie said.

We did just that as Albert and Rose stared. Charlie clipped Albert on the back of his head.

"What, you never saw a kid before?"

"Not a softwire, Charlie."

"Sorry, honey," Rose said, smiling at me. "It's been pretty boring for us lately."

"She's right. Tell us everything. How are your Guarantors?" Albert asked.

"Mine hates me," I said.

"Mine's dead," Max said.

"Oh my," Rose responded. "And what about yours, sweetheart?" Rose leaned toward Ketheria and put her hand on her head. Ketheria pulled her head back and snuggled toward me.

"She can't talk," I told them. "She's been that way since she was born."

"How about a nice glass of Coca-Cola? That will clear the pipes and get her talking," said Charlie, punching some buttons on an O-dat at the table. Three large glasses filled with a brown, fizzy liquid materialized on the table.

"Go on, try it."

We each took a glass and sipped. Max sprayed hers all over Albert.

"Yuck! What is this stuff?" Max asked.

"International drink of Earth. First company to sponsor a seed-ship to another galaxy."

"It makes my eyes water," Theodore said.

"Your sister doesn't seem to mind it," Rose pointed out.

Albert was still wiping his glasses off. Ketheria had almost finished her entire glass. She seemed to be enjoying it quite a bit. She finished hers and was reaching for mine when she let out a loud burp.

"There's a good earthling," Charlie said, laughing.

I liked Charlie and his friends. They made me laugh, too. Albert was always doing something silly, and soon even Ketheria was smiling. When Charlie mentioned the disaster at the Science and Research building, we told them everything. We told them about the Neewalkers, the slopcrawler, and the strange city of Keepers.

"That's Magna," Charlie said.

"It was once the city of the Ancients," Albert said.

"Now the Keepers live below it," Charlie added.

"Someone got us out of there," I said. "I don't know who, but it wasn't any Citizen; they think I'm somehow involved with the central computer."

"Just like them," Albert said. "Always trying to

find a way to get folks off the rings. Want to keep the riches for themselves."

"Let 'em have them," Rose said.

"Won't be much left anyway if they don't figure out what's wrong with Big Bertha," Albert said.

"Big Bertha?" Max said.

"Albert works in maintenance. That's what he calls the central computer. He gets to hear about all the little glitches that have been happening before anyone else," Charlie said.

Albert held up the vest he was wearing. It was similar to the skins we wore for Weegin's World, but an official digital ID badge was sewn in and blue piping ran along the edges.

"There have been more?" I asked him.

"Oh yeah. Little things everywhere, but they keep it quiet because it will scare the heckers out of the Citizens. I say, tell them everything and let's figure out what's wrong before it's too late," Albert said.

"What do they think is causing it?" Max asked.

"Not a clue," said Albert. "But I think —"

"Don't start your doomsday talk, Albert. That's all you talk about. Besides, those Neewalkers scare me," Rose said.

"She's right: let it go," Charlie said. "Another soda for everyone?"

Ketheria was the only one who accepted Charlie's offer. I had never seen her this happy before. I didn't want the spoke to end. I don't know why, but I felt comfortable. Maybe this was all there was supposed to be: good friends, something to talk about, nothing more. I made a point not to think about it. I wanted to enjoy myself, too. I didn't know how long this would last or if it would ever happen again.

Before we left, Charlie, Albert, and Rose invited us to join them at the Earth News Café whenever we wanted.

"We're always here. Don't be shy," Albert shouted as we waved good-bye. Ketheria chased her glowglobes all the way back to Weegin's World.

I said good night to Max and Ketheria and went to my room. I was feeling content for the first time since I arrived on Orbis. *See, it just took a little time,* I told myself. I wanted more of this, and I knew it was up to me to find it. I looked at the dream-enhancement headset and put it on. Nothing was going to stop me from enjoying my new home now. I set the dials for color: low; sound: soft; characters: random. I adjusted the headset and closed my eyes.

Within moments I was wandering through the clouds as if I could fly. Soft music filtered down from above me, and a peaceful feeling breezed through my body. I was high above Weegin's World on Orbis 1 and the magnificent ring curved up around me on both sides. I could see the lights from the other towns and cities, as well as large bodies of water on the surface of the ring. It was beautiful. I followed the water to Magna.

Waterfalls surrounded the ancient city and the huge red birds circled high above. I was not afraid of them this time, and I floated down toward them. Soon, I was flying next to them. They beat their giant wings, and one turned to look at me. Its eyes glittered a bright gold, reflecting the distant sunlight, but there was no threat in them now.

I almost passed her before a shimmer caught my attention. Far below me, behind a building on the outskirts of Magna, appeared the little girl I once mistook for Ketheria. She was dismantling a wall panel attached to the structure. I circled above the little girl without her knowing. She plucked knobs and controls from the panel, jumping back sometimes as sparks flew. After digging awhile, she removed an instrument plate and threw it onto the ground.

She's looking for something to play with, I thought. I reached into my pocket and found a lost glowglobe I had retrieved for Ketheria. It was still with me in my dream. I drifted lower and dropped the globe. It bounced erratically in front of the little girl, making her jump back. The ball returned to me when my feet touched the ground. The little girl looked up and bolted when she saw me. I stayed and bounced the ball again.

After a moment the little girl peeked out from behind the wall. I ignored her but kept making the glowglobe move in all different directions while the little girl watched. Slowly she moved out from behind the wall and tried to pluck the ball from the air whenever it bounced near her. Soon the little girl was jumping and laughing with every attempt to catch the ball.

I moved a little closer.

She almost caught the ball, and giggled with delight. I bounced the ball a little higher, and she lifted herself off the ground to try to reach it. Despite her ability to cause terror, as she chased after the jumping sphere, the little girl seemed as harmless as Ketheria.

I inched nearer.

I was close now. The little girl's skin flickered lightly in the sun. I could see computer code running under her skin like blood through a vein. Her eyes were the color of a computer chip, and I even thought I could see the circuitry. She pushed her brown hair away from her face. It gave off an unusual sheen, almost plasticlike, and it did not react to the wind.

I caught the ball as the little girl turned. We stood toe to toe.

"Hi," I said, and smiled.

For a moment I thought the little girl might actually respond. Instead, her eyes glowed bright white and I was instantly transported to the same scorching, barren planet that she had sent me to once before. This time, however, I was tied to the ground. I could feel the sizzling surface burning my back. I let out a scream, but no one could hear me. My wrists were chained to sticks in the ground and the giant red birds circled above, patiently waiting for their dinner to cook.

I woke still screaming, but it hardly disturbed

anyone. Switzer grunted and rolled over. I removed the headset and this time I ripped it from the sleeper, destroying it. I would pay whatever Weegin deducted from my pittance for the damage.
I lay back down, but something jabbed into my ribs. It was a small screen scroll. I pushed the lid back and opened the tiny message.

> Meet me at the Earth News Café, recreation spoke, next cycle.
> Tell no one.
>
> Theylor

Tell no one? What did this mean? Why didn't Theylor come to me straightaway? Why was he being so secretive? I put my head on the pillow, but any sleep was now impossible.

15

"Why do you think the little girl in your dreams has something to do with the computer malfunctions?" Max asked while I helped Ketheria onto the spaceway.

"I don't think she has *something* to do with it; I think she *is* doing it. All of it," I said.

"How does the computer not recognize her, then?"

"Maybe the Trading Council put her in there and she's under their control," I suggested.

"Maybe the Keepers put her in there," Max replied.

"I don't know what to think anymore, but I do know I always see her doing a lot of damage," I said.

"But you never see her doing the damage at hand. Maybe it is just a dream," she said.

"Then how do you explain my seeing her when I enter the computer?"

Max looked out the window at the crystal moons. "Your guess is as good as mine."

I used my social studies class to get as much information as I could before meeting with Theylor. By pushing into the central computer, I was able to bypass the alarm Keetle used to keep us from studying anything she did not want us to learn. I made Max and Theodore stand guard in case Keetle snuck up on me.

Once inside, I learned that the Neewalkers were a dangerous breed but not very loyal. During their history of criminal employment, they had switched alliances several times, always to the highest bidder. Whoever had hired the Neewalkers was very wealthy. Money was the only way to ensure their loyalty.

"Only the Trading Council or its Guarantors could afford that," I said.

"Or Keepers," Max said.

"I don't think so. Look at this."

I showed her a digi of Sar Cyrillus. Standing behind him was the Guarantor Torlee.

"Torlee?"

"It says Torlee used to be a Trading Council member."

"He looks awfully friendly with that Neewalker," I said.

"What does it mean?"

"I don't know, but it's the only connection I can find."

I also learned that Neewalkers were permitted on the Rings of Orbis. No one was barred from visiting Orbis, since it did not have planetary status. No one, that is, except Space Jumpers, and they seemed to have no problem at all moving around Orbis 1. The Keepers only controlled who lived on Orbis and who landed on the crystal moons. That's why the Trading Council had to deal with the Keepers when it came to harvesting and profiting from the crystals.

"None of this helps us very much," Theodore said.

"I know to stay away from these guys," Max said as Keetle shut down the O-dats to end the session.

"C'mon. I think we should tell Boohral's kid what we know," I said.

"Why?" Max grabbed Ketheria and followed.

"If it was me, I'd want to know."

"I'm going back," Theodore said. "Weegin will freak if I'm not there. You, too, Max."

"We won't be long," she said. "Make an excuse for us."

We jumped a chute to the Citizen level, only to be greeted by sneers from the other kids. Max spotted the big Trefaldoor.

"Graalon," Max called out, but Graalon showed no intention of talking to a group of knudniks, especially in front of everyone. "Graalon, wait."

"You shouldn't be up here. This is for Citizens, not knudniks," Graalon said with a snarl. He looked just like his father, only smaller — but not much smaller.

"We have information about your father," I blurted out.

Graalon looked around and then said, "Follow me."

The huge alien led us to a room off the top floor of the social studies cylinder. Drones flew back and forth, replenishing food and drink while Citizens lay around on loungers much nicer than the ones in Weegin's World.

"What are you doing bringing knudniks in here, Graalon?" demanded one alien, a slender creature with soft emerald skin. Its movements reminded me of a plant swaying gracefully in the wind, but its voice was full of thorns.

"This one belonged to my father. The other is the human Softwire. Leave us be, Dop," Graalon growled.

The sight of the large yellow alien leaning against the frail greenish one made me smirk, something I shouldn't have done. Dop moved swiftly toward me, grabbed me by the throat, and lifted me off my feet.

"Do you find me funny, knudnik?" Dop said through clenched teeth.

"Put him down!" Max yelled. "Graalon, stop him!" But Graalon just moved toward a tray of toonbas while I dangled in Dop's grip.

"You're not welcome on Orbis. You'll never be welcome on Orbis." Dop's breath smelled like flowers, only rotting ones. I stared at the alien, not willing to show any fear. A toonba flew across the room and hit Dop in the head. Ketheria was winding up to launch another when Graalon grunted at Dop.

"Remember what I said," Dop whispered as he dropped me.

I sat on the floor, rubbing my neck as the alien left, then got up and joined Graalon, Max, and

Ketheria.

"Why are the Citizens so against us being here? No one is really from here," I said.

Graalon plopped his large fleshy body on a lounger. A small round metal disc like his father's hovered over his head, only fewer wires were attached. Graalon shared a bowl of toonbas with Ketheria. Graalon seemed to take a liking to Ketheria, who shared his appreciation for the Trefaldoorian treat.

"The universe is very old, Softwire," he said. "Humans have existed for only a brief moment on the timeline of life. Most of the Citizens on the Rings of Orbis have no home planet anymore. It has been swallowed by a dying sun, has been destroyed by warfare, or has succumbed to elements out of their control. Orbis is their sanctuary, a chance for a new future for their kind. They do not want it overtaken by unworthy species, ones that would abandon a perfectly good planet instead of fixing it or that would trade their time for a place on the rings. Time is too precious to trade away. We find humans weak and useless. They have no purpose here. I doubt you could understand the deep feelings of the Citizens."

I thought about Earth, a planet I would never know, and about my parents, who gave their lives trying to get here.

"No, Graalon, you're wrong. I understand it completely."

"Then you'll appreciate their resentment," he

replied.

"I am willing to try."

"Good. Now what is this information you have about my father?"

Max and I told Graalon that we had met his father's slopcrawler, and we described the attack by the Neewalkers.

"Neewalkers! So my father was right." Graalon tapped on an O-dat. "Where is this slopcrawler now? We need him to testify in front of the council." Graalon labored to his feet. "Take me to him."

"We can't," I said.

"We don't know where he is," Max added, trying to soften the truth.

"He could be dead. He was left with the Neewalkers." I was not as sensitive.

Max gave me a wide-eyed stare.

"So what are we going to do?" I said.

"We? This is none of your concern, knudnik," Graalon said.

Now I was on my feet. "It *is* my concern. We were nearly killed, let alone the fact that a war would not make Orbis a nice place for any species."

Graalon sat back at his O-dat. "The Keepers are trying to remove the Trading Council from power. They want to control the profits from the crystal moons. They are sabotaging the computer to squeeze the Trading Council out."

"The Keepers believe the Trading Council is responsible for the central computer malfunctioning," I informed him.

"Why would we destroy our own businesses? They are our only way of life."

"Why would the Keepers risk destroying something they were born to protect?" I shot back.

"Religion."

"What do you mean?" I said.

"The Keepers live more by a religion than a philosophy, especially the old ones. They feel some sort of connection to the Ancients and to a prophecy that their race failed to live up to a long time ago. But still they want to bring back the benevolence of the Ancients and make the crystal-moon harvests free to everyone again."

"We overheard Drapling say that in the city of Keepers," Max said.

"It's ridiculous. Just because the Ancients were brainless doesn't mean we have to be. That wealth is my birthright now." Graalon mumbled the last words. "Wait, you were inside Magna?"

"Yeah. If Magna is where the Keepers live."

"I don't believe you — how did you get there?"

"A Space Jumper left us near there," I said.

"Now you really are lying to me. The council banned Space Jumpers almost a millennium ago. A Trefaldoor can smell a lie. You would have to summon the Space Jumper. Only Keepers and their own kind can summon a Space Jumper," Graalon said as a look of contempt washed across his puny face.

We had already stayed too long. Theodore would not be able to make excuses for us for much longer. "We have to go," I told Max.

"Graalon, a lot of strange things are happening on Orbis 1," she said. "We're telling the truth. Everything we've told you is the truth."

"We only want to protect Orbis 1. It's our home, too, whether you like it or not," I said.

"I wish some of the Citizens felt the way you do, earthling."

When we arrived at Weegin's World, the hover belts were turned off and the giant crane robots hung motionless from the ceiling. I headed straight for my room, eager to get to the Earth News Café.

"Where are you off to?" Weegin barked when he saw me bolt for the door.

"The hover belts are down," I replied, pointing to the silent machines.

"Cleaning time."

"What?" Switzer didn't like the sound of that, either.

Weegin made us clean every nut and every single bolt of the hover belts. The grease, combined with the evil-smelling radiation gel, added up to a thoroughly nasty job.

"Don't rush out of here after work, JT; we want to go, too," Max said, and Ketheria nodded in agreement.

"I have to go by myself — sorry," I said.

"What do you mean?" Max was offended.

"I just . . . I just have to go alone. Okay? Just this time."

"Can I come?" Theodore said, eavesdropping on our conversation.

"No!" I snapped.

"Sorry for asking."

"No, I'm sorry. I . . . this, um — I need to . . ."

"What are you up to now, Softwire? Get back to work. Or do you want to spend the next spoke here, too?" Weegin said, which only made me very nervous. I didn't want anything to go wrong.

"Nothing," I replied, and turned to Theodore. "Next time, okay? I promise."

"Fine," Max said.

I just shrugged and went back to cleaning the grime off the belts — anything to pass the time.

When the spoke was finally finished, I quickly cleaned up and headed for the door while Max and Theodore ignored me. Ketheria hurried next to me.

"No. Stay with Max, Ketheria."

She looked at me for a moment, then headed for the door as though I had said nothing.

"Ketheria, no."

"Ketheria! Over here. C'mon, let him do whatever he wants," Max called.

While I sat on the spaceway feeling a little guilty for the way I had treated my friends, I asked myself a very hard question: *What are you trying to do?* One moment I felt excited at the thought of my life on Orbis and my new friends. But the very next moment my body filled with anxiety about the Citizens' accusations. I really just wanted it all to go away. I'd accepted the fact that I was a slave on

Orbis and that nothing could change that. All I wanted was to serve out my time on Orbis and maybe create a place for my sister and me. Could Theylor help me? All I could do was ask.

I made my way through the Trading Hall and entered the Earth News Café. Theylor was waiting for me in the same booth where I had met Charlie and his pals, although this time there was no sign of my Earth friends. Theylor nodded his right head when he saw me.

"I am glad to see you are all right," said Theylor, rising as I slid into the booth. "Would you like something to eat?"

"No, thanks, I'm fine."

"Are you really?"

"Everything lately has been pretty crazy, to be honest. I mean, I'm seeing Space Jumpers and they're supposed to be banished. The central computer's going crazy. My dreams are more like nightmares. Yeah, maybe things aren't all right."

"Were any of you hurt at the Center for Science and Research?"

"No, but I still don't know how —"

"How you escaped the dark-matter containment room?"

"The what?"

"The Ancients used dark matter to stabilize the wormhole. An amplifier in the room creates the extraordinary mass Orbis needs to keep the wormhole open. It also creates the energy needed to maintain each ring's photonic gravity reactor.

You're lucky you didn't die in there."

"You got us out?"

Theylor nodded. "That will be our secret," he said.

"This is all crazy for me, Theylor."

"There is a very serious threat to the existence of Orbis right now, Johnny," he said, lowering his voice.

"Why are you telling me this? I'm just a piece of property, right?"

"I am aware of your status, but your existence is still very important."

"Why?"

"The Keepers have always been protected by the Space Jumpers. They fought the War of Ten Thousand Rotations with us and created a stable environment for everyone on Orbis."

"What went wrong?"

"The Keepers are not very good at business. If some Keepers had it their way, they would give the crystals away for free. For them, to give is the ultimate achievement. The problem, however, is that the financial transactions of Orbis need better guidance in order to maintain everything you see around you."

"And that's where the Trading Council comes in."

"Precisely," he said. "The Citizens are brilliant at managing the resources of the crystal moons. When peace was made after the War of Ten Thousand Rotations and the Keepers allowed the

Citizens to inhabit the rings, the Trading Council was formed to oversee all business functions. But the Space Jumpers had fought for our side and their presence offended the Citizens. Some had altercations with Jumpers in different galaxies. Some Citizens, I'm afraid, are not very honest."

"So they made you get rid of the Space Jumpers?"

"When the Trading Council proved their worth and created the unimaginable wealth that we now have, they became very powerful. Orbis became dependent on the constant guidance of the Trading Council. We were forced to listen to them."

"So you banished the Space Jumpers from Orbis — you turned your backs on the people who protected you for thousands and thousands of years."

Theylor bowed both heads in shame. "I am afraid that is correct, but we still remain in constant contact with them."

"That's obvious. But what does all of this have to do with me?"

"All Space Jumpers are softwires. They could protect the central computer from sabotage or outside attack, but they could also access it at will. This was also one of the reasons they made the Citizens so nervous. They didn't want anyone poking around inside their computer like that."

"But that's what you think is happening now?"

"Yes. We believe someone in the Trading Council is manipulating the central computer, but we have no way of proving this. We cannot use a Space Jumper to protect the computer without breaking our agreement with the Council."

"Didn't you break the Council's agreement by working with the Space Jumpers at all?"

"Space Jumpers have intervened only in matters of life and death. Otherwise we have only counseled with them. Putting them in control of the central computer would be a direct breach of our agreement."

"But Theylor, I don't think the Council is controlling the computer. I think it's a virus."

Theylor seemed confused.

"I am sorry, Johnny, but that is just not possible," Theylor said, shaking his heads.

"But it's true; I've seen it!"

"When?"

"In my dreams when I hook up to the dream-enhancement equipment, or whenever I go deep into the computer. I saw it walk straight through the security seal that you were so proud of. It didn't even stop. I never told you because I didn't think you would believe me."

"You should have spoken of this earlier. If this is true, then the council has created something that will truly threaten the existence of Orbis. If they can control the central computer, they will control us."

Theylor tapped on the O-dat at the table and bypassed the menu. More strange symbols formed on the screen, which I recognized as the Keepers' language. He worked with the screen as I just sat and watched him. Finally, I broke the silence.

"You still haven't explained how this involves me."

Theylor looked up. "You can enter the computer for us and protect it from the Council, even more than a Space Jumper. You can act as our final defense."

I didn't want to be involved, but this seemed like a simple task. "That's not a big deal," I said. "I can do it during my rec spoke."

In fact, I actually liked the idea of having something important to do on Orbis, and it would give me time to prove them wrong and expose the virus.

"It's not as simple as that," Theylor said. "You would have to be in the computer longer than your recreational spoke."

"You'll have to take that up with Weegin. I don't mind getting out of a few work spokes."

"I'm afraid you don't understand. We want you to live inside the computer."

"What do you mean? Forever? Always? Could I come out and see Ketheria?"

"I am afraid not. Once you've disconnected from your physical existence, your body will die shortly after."

"No way, Theylor. I'm sorry, but no way."

Theylor just continued to look at me. I had come here because I thought he was going to help me. But something on his face told me otherwise.

"I don't have a choice, do I? You're only here to

warn me," I said.

I stared in disbelief as Theylor nodded both his heads.

"Drapling is preparing the outline of the decree as we speak. There is talk of war, and the Keepers must move swiftly."

This was not happening. "What if I run away?" I asked him. "Yes, you could help me, Theylor. Please. I could escape. I'll go far away from here. I'll take Ketheria with me."

"You asked about this when you first arrived. I'm afraid if you run, the punishment would still be the same."

"You mean death?"

Theylor nodded his heads again. I couldn't believe what I was hearing. The café was spinning around me.

"How long do I have?" I asked him.

"Three or four cycles, maybe. No more than a phase, I am afraid. This should be enough time to put your affairs in order," Theylor said.

"My affairs!" I stood up. "This is a death sentence. You want me to go around and tell everyone good-bye? See ya later? Look me up on an O-dat every once in a while!"

I sat back down hard. In my pocket was the makeshift locket Ketheria had given me. I pulled out the pictures of my parents and stared at their faces locked inside the organic polymer. *Is this what they wanted for me?* I just wouldn't believe it.

"I do not comprehend your level of anger,"

Theylor said. "You still have your debt to pay to Orbis."

"With my life? No one said I had to pay with my life."

"You will still be able to communicate with others that connect with the computer, and you will have a rewarding life guarding the sanctity of Orbis 1," Theylor offered.

I put the picture back in my pocket and leaned over the table. "I hate to be the one to inform you, but I really don't care about Orbis right now. I don't care about you or the Keepers or the stupid deal they made with the Trading Council. I know most people around here don't think a human is worth much, but I do. Figure something else out!"

I stormed out of the Earth News Café and ran straight into Charlie, Albert, and Rose.

"Whoa there, big fella. What's the rush?" Charlie said.

I didn't say anything, just walked around them. Ketheria was standing behind them with Max and Theodore.

I picked up my pace and walked through the Trading Hall. I never looked back, but I knew my friends would follow. I didn't know if I wanted them there or not. I didn't know anything at that moment. Nothing made sense. Nothing mattered. Everything was out of focus inside my head.

"JT, wait up! Please!" Max yelled.

I turned around. Albert and Rose were gone, but Charlie was with Ketheria and my friends. They stood there, with the green and blue lights from the trading chambers bouncing off the back of their heads, staring at me like I was an alien. My stomach flipped. I did not want to leave them.

"What's the big rush?" Max said, catching up to me.

"Nothing. I . . . I didn't see you there." I swallowed hard. I did not want them to see me cry.

"Is everything all right, son?" Charlie asked. Ketheria took my hand. I did not want to look her in the eyes.

"Charlie showed us some really awesome places in the trading chambers," Theodore said. "You've got to see them."

"Sure, maybe next phase." *If I'm not living in the central computer by then*, I thought.

"Are you sure you're all right? Come on back to the café. Albert has some funny stories about Big Bertha. He spends a lot of time trying to crack those ones and zeros," Charlie said.

"I really just want to go home. Maybe you're right, I'm . . ."

Ketheria looked at me strangely. She squeezed my hand tighter.

"What did you say?" I asked Charlie.

"The ones and zeros, computer code — old computer code. It's a joke. Not like the computer here on Orbis, which works with light, but, you know, like the computers back home."

"Some central-computer functions still use binary code," Theodore interrupted.

"I'm sure they do," said Charlie, "but on Earth everything was based on ones and zeros."

"Like the number ten?" I said.

"Well, a little, in the sense that a one next to a zero looks like a ten, but I mean —"

"What are you getting at?" Max said.

I was dumbfounded. Why hadn't I seen this before? She had left it right in front of me.

"The little girl in my dream. I always see the number ten," I whispered to Max.

"You all right, Johnny?" Charlie asked again.

But my mind was going a kilometer a second. It took everything just to stand up.

The little girl was trying to tell me something.

At first I refused Charlie's offer of walking us to the spaceway, but Charlie would not take no for an answer.

"The dark brings out a whole new breed of aliens," Charlie cautioned. "Besides, I have to take the spaceway anyway."

I could tell by the look on Ketheria's face that Charlie was fibbing. All I need to do is look at Ketheria to know if someone is lying. She has a knack for smelling an untruth, but we let Charlie walk with us all the same. Besides, Max and Ketheria enjoyed his company. They loved his crazy stories about that funny town called Chicago. And I needed time to think.

Night on Orbis is only a little darker than the day. As we walked to the spaceway, I concentrated on the stars in the deepest corner of the universe. I wondered how much longer I would get to see them.

"Are you thinking about the little girl in your dreams?" Theodore asked, breaking my trance. I glared at Max, who shrugged sheepishly.

"I might have mentioned something," she said, looking away.

"Having bad dreams, are we, son?" Charlie asked.

"JT thinks there is someone in the computer causing the problems, not the Keepers or the Trading Council," Theodore said.

"The computer would identify any foreign code and assimilate it or destroy it," Charlie said. "The computer's been around a helluva long time. It knows a lot."

"Can it know everything, though?" I asked. "I mean, could there be something it doesn't know? Someone or something?"

"I don't know how," he said.

Charlie helped Ketheria into the spaceway. She had done it so many times now I think she only let people help her for the attention.

"You know, Johnny, the Keepers and the Citizens have been going at it for some time. Especially the Trading Council. I don't know of anything the computer did not catch. If there's something or someone messing with it, it has to be one of those two," Charlie said, as the spaceway headed toward Weegin's World.

"Don't you live the other way, Charlie?"

Theodore asked.

"That's all right, I've got nothing to do anyway."

I trusted Charlie, but something in my stomach told me he was wrong. When I was on the *Renaissance,* some of the kids did not believe that the computer could talk to me, and I had put up with years of abuse from people like Switzer and Dalton. It was the same thing now. I knew what I'd seen — I just needed to prove it.

16

Charlie rode with us all the way back to Weegin's World. Ketheria gave Charlie a hug before he left, and Max promised we'd come back to the café on our next rec cycle.

"You're gonna come, too, right?" he said to me.

"Sure," I told him.

Charlie put his hand on my shoulder and said, "You may not see it right now, Johnny, but our presence here is good for mankind. There's no way our species will survive if humans don't head to the stars like we did. Think of us as pioneers."

I looked up at Charlie as he stood tall and puffed out his chest, trying to make me laugh. I wanted to tell him about how the Keepers were going to make me live inside the central computer and I would never see any of them again. I wanted to ask him if I could escape from the ring. I wanted help, but I didn't want any more people involved.

"Promise me you'll come by tomorrow," Charlie said. "For me."

"I will. Thanks, Charlie," I said, and headed inside.

We entered the first interior dome with little fanfare. As usual, our vests automatically granted us access through the door. We walked under the warm yellow light that illuminated the foyer, and crossed the walkway high above the sorting-bay floor.

"I thought Weegin might lock us out," Max said.

"No, he'd just deduct chits from us," Theodore said.

None of it mattered to me anymore.

Max tapped on the control panel that activated the energy beam that served as the walkway. The blue light beam shot across the sorting bay and connected to the other side. Even at this late hour the robotic cranes continued to work as we crossed.

That's when I heard a scream.

"What was that, JT?" Theodore asked. Ketheria snuggled close to me.

"I think it was Weegin."

"Look," Max said, pointing up several levels to Weegin's office, perched high above the factory.

"He's not alone," I said.

I could see Weegin's silhouette through the office glass. Three other figures stood next to him. One held Weegin up as he kicked his feet in the air. The shapes of the other figures were undeniable.

"That's a Neewalker with him," Max said. "Let's get out of here."

Max and Ketheria both started back across the walkway.

"We can't," I said, and moved toward the elevator shaft.

"Johnny, this is not our fight. Let Weegin handle his own shady deals," Theodore said.

"It's my fight, too, I'm afraid. More than you

know. The ring is in trouble, and whether I like it or not — whether *we* like it or not — I have to help him," I told them. "Maybe you can take Ketheria back to her room."

"You don't know that this has to do with the central computer, JT. Weegin could be up to no good all on his own," Max said.

"She's right," Theodore added.

I looked at Ketheria, but she shook her head. I knew that whatever Weegin was up to somehow involved me.

"The whole time we were on the *Renaissance,* I dreamed about living on Orbis. I thought of nothing else. But we don't have a hope of making a good life here unless I can prove there's a virus in the central computer. The Citizens and the Keepers are convinced it's each other, and they're willing to take extreme measures to prove it."

"What extreme measures?" Theodore asked.

"I'm going to do this with or without you," I said.

"No. If you go, we all go," Max said, and Theodore nodded.

With a deep breath and a lot of apprehension, I headed for the elevator door.

None of us had ever used Weegin's elevator or entered Weegin's office before. We tried to be as quiet as possible, but the elevator screeched as it lifted us to Weegin's level. If we had hoped for an element of surprise, we had definitely lost it.

"I don't like this, JT," Max said.

"Me neither, but when that door opens, get ready to duck under the stilts of the Neewalkers. That will give me enough time to access the chip and knock them over."

"You're kidding, right?" Max said.

"No, I'm not."

Theodore kept mumbling as he stared at the door.

"What are you doing?" Max asked him.

"He's counting," I said. "It calms him down."

"Counting what?" she asked.

"My heartbeats," he replied.

The elevator rose at a deathly slow pace, centimeter by centimeter. When the door finally disappeared, Ketheria panicked. She grabbed my vest and yanked me to the back of the lift. She got in front of me and punched at the controls.

"Ketheria, I have to," I said, trying to calm her, but it was no use. She was frantically trying to get the elevator to go back down.

"Ketheria?" Max said.

"Look, no one is there," I said when the lift stopped, but that didn't stop Ketheria. She would not let me leave the elevator.

"Ketheria, I must do this now. C'mon — please," I said as I fought her off and headed for Weegin's office.

A familiar sound came from behind us.

I turned to find Sar Cyrillus poised with a large ion rifle aimed right at us.

"Surprised?" he asked.

I immediately accessed the chip that controlled Sar Cyrillus's mechanical legs.

"Don't bother, Softwire. You can only do that to us once."

He was right. I immediately encountered a blocking device that would take some time to figure out.

"Get your dirty little mind out of my computer chip," he said, shifting toward us. "And get a move on."

Sar Cyrillus motioned toward the office with the giant weapon that extended from his right arm. No one argued, and I took the lead.

I reached for the door to Weegin's office, and Ketheria tugged my arm again.

"I know. Stay close," I said. I looked at her. She shook her head very slowly, almost as if she was trying to tell me she was sorry — for what, I didn't know.

"No, it's my fault, Ketheria. Maybe I should have listened."

The door disappeared.

"It's about time. I didn't know Weegin let his chattel stay out so long. I would not have come so early," a familiar voice said from the shadows.

Madame Lee stepped out from the corner of Weegin's office.

"You?" I stared at Madame Lee. Her jet-black skin and pure white hair were a stark contrast to knobby little Weegin, who hung in the air, thanks to the meanest-looking Neewalker I'd ever seen. Another Neewalker stood in the corner.

"Don't look so surprised. I might be offended," she said, pushing a braid behind her long, thin ears.

Ketheria moved behind me, trying to stay out of Madame Lee's sight. Madame Lee set her piercing silver pupils on Theodore.

"Who's this?" she asked, and she snuck a peek at Ketheria. When Madame Lee moved closer to Theodore, Ketheria moved behind Max.

"I'm Theodore."

"Yes, you are, and you're wishing you hadn't invited yourself on their little excursion, aren't you?"

"How did you know?" he said.

"I know a lot of things."

Sar Cyrillus grew impatient. "Get on with this," he growled, and Weegin squirmed in the hands of the ugly Neewalker.

"Put me down," he demanded.

"Be quiet, worm," Madame Lee snapped.

I tried to push into the computer chips of the other Neewalkers, but they were also using the blocking device.

"Poor child," Madame Lee said, obviously knowing what I was trying to do. "Do you think the Trading Council succeeds without any defense against those Space Jumpers and that nasty little habit of yours? How could we do our business if we didn't know how to shut those meddling creatures out of our computers?"

"Why are you trying to destroy the central computer? It's only going to ruin Orbis," Max demanded.

Madame Lee let out a deep breath. "Oh, ignorant little one. We are not destroying the computer; the Keepers are. They're greedier than we are, if you can believe that."

"Not really," I said.

"Well, they are. They want those beautiful moons all to themselves, and I will not allow that. Were it not for that idiot Trefaldoor, everything would be mine by now."

"Boohral?" I said.

"Yes, that oversize, bloated yellow do-gooder. How can a Trefaldoor be expected to do business for us? Trefaldoors, poor things, are biologically unable to lie, and lying is essential to our success." She grinned.

"So is killing," Max said, but the comment didn't even faze Madame Lee. She smiled at Ketheria. A knowing smile I couldn't figure out.

"Unfortunately, you're right. But it was so easy to disguise. The creatures on this ring will believe anything they see as long as it comes from that stupid central computer. And that brings us to how we're going to deal with you meddlesome brats. Especially you." She pointed at me. "There is no way I'm going to let the Keepers put you into the computer to spy on us. If they're going to waste your talents by making you live in the central computer, I would rather see you dead."

"What?" Theodore said.

Max and Theodore looked at me. Ketheria could not hold back her tears.

"Is that true, JT?" Max asked.

"It certainly is," Madame Lee replied. "The Keepers, those two-headed know-it-alls you admire so much, have condemned your little friend to a life of servitude inside the central computer. Isn't that nice?"

"Well, I'm not doing it," I said.

"Oh, but you know the penalty if you don't obey your owners. You're dead either way, I'm afraid."

"Weegin, is this true?" Max asked.

Weegin dropped his head.

"Don't worry. Weegin will be paid handsomely for his loss." Madame Lee smiled. "He's been planning to sell you off from the very beginning."

"Don't kill them all," Weegin said. "That's almost half my stock."

"*Your* stock? Remember, I own you, too, now. I'm not going to kill anyone — yet."

"How do you know about the Keepers' wanting Johnny to live in the computer?" Max said.

An evil grin spread across Madame Lee's face. "Powerful friends in powerful places? I mean, how can I have any control over their precious computer if I don't know about their security devices?"

Madame Lee drifted toward Ketheria. Ketheria would not look at her.

"What's the matter, my child? Still trying to

hide your secret?" she said in a motherly voice. Ketheria just stared at her feet.

"What secret?" I asked, trying to position myself between Madame Lee and my sister.

"Quite a big secret. A secret she discovered on the *Renaissance* but was afraid to tell her brother once she read about how they treated telepaths on Orbis. Aren't I correct, dear?"

Madame Lee stroked Ketheria's hair as Ketheria stared at me.

"Telepath?" Max and I said in unison. Theodore simply stared with his mouth open.

"I have a softwire *and* a telepath?" Weegin said.

"Shut up," Madame Lee scolded him. She turned back to me. "Your little sister has the ability to read minds. She actually prefers it to talking. I'm sure she could talk if she wanted to. Isn't that right?" But Ketheria did not respond.

This definitely explained a lot of things about my sister.

Ketheria pointed at Madame Lee. I understood immediately.

"You're a telepath, too!" I exclaimed.

Madame Lee only smiled. "Getting smarter by the moment."

"Why didn't you let me know, Ketheria?" I asked her.

Max knelt next to Ketheria. "She couldn't, JT. All telepaths must report to security upon their arrival. It's one of the Keepers' decrees. First they are quarantined, and then they are fitted with a device to control their abilities," Max said.

"Your little sister would have been taken away once you arrived. Who would have wanted that?" Madame Lee added.

"If you're a telepath, how come you're not registered? How come you're not wearing a device that lets everyone else know?" Max asked.

"I made them write the decree, of course, a very, very long time ago. Besides, how do you think I find them? But now the truth must be told."

Madame Lee reached into her tight-fitting outfit, a combination of leather padding and something that resembled turtle shells or reptile scales. She removed a communication device and spoke into it: "This is Councilwoman Lee. I must report an unregistered telepath. I'm requesting an immediate self-guiding security sphere. Direct it to these coordinates."

"No!" I screamed, but before I could even move, Ketheria was sealed in a green security bubble like the one they had used on me. I could see Ketheria pounding on the inside of the bubble, but no one could help her. I tried to grab the bubble. Max and Theodore tried, too, as Madame Lee and the Neewalkers laughed. I knew from experience it was no use. The bubble left Weegin's World with Ketheria inside.

"If you ever want her back, you must do exactly as I say," Madame Lee said.

"What do you want me to do?" I demanded.

"That's better," she said with a smile. "First,

we'll deal with this."

Madame Lee pulled out a computer drive. I could not hide the surprise on my face. It was the same computer drive Boohral had revealed at the tribunal. Could it be the one that contained the restricted files from the *Renaissance*?

"Cost me a Trefaldoor to finally get my hands on this," Madame Lee said.

"You're a murderer," Max said, spitting out the words.

"Such name calling," Madame Lee said. "Is that really necessary?" Madame Lee looked at me. "You're dying to know what's on this, aren't you, my boy?"

"Not really," I said.

Madame Lee snapped back, "Have you not been paying attention? I've been listening to you think about this meddlesome hunk of metal since the moment I pulled it out. Do not underestimate me, Softwire."

Madame Lee tossed me the drive. I stared at it in my hands. I wanted desperately to know what was on it.

"I know you do," she said. "Now throw it out the window."

"What?" I said. I couldn't; there was no way. Here it was, right in my hands. I tried to push into it, but there was no power source. *What's going on here?* my mind screamed.

"Fine, we'll do it the hard way." Madame Lee motioned to the Neewalker, who grabbed Max, lifted her off the floor, and moved toward the open window.

"Wait!" I needed more time. I looked around the room.

"It's either her or that meddlesome little device. It's your choice," she said.

There was no choice. I looked at Max. I had hoped there was some secret, some clue my parents had tucked away in these files, but I was not willing to risk Max's life for it.

"You think all your answers are in that, don't you, earthling? Maybe an answer for why you and your sister are what you are?" Madame Lee walked to the window. "You've been asking the wrong question, my son. I'm afraid the answers on this drive are to questions I do not want asked."

"But —"

"Oh, this is so boring. Toss her over."

"All right!"

I tossed the drive out the window. It sailed out of Weegin's office and smashed on the factory floor. Weegin's robotic scavengers scurried out and gobbled up the pieces. I had been so close to finding out the answers to everything, but nothing could bring that drive back now. I felt like I had watched someone die right before my eyes.

"I hate you," I said to her.

"You wouldn't be the first," she replied.

"Why do you care about that drive?" I asked. Madame Lee laughed.

"Now that the drive is gone and it would only

be the word of a slave against mine, I will tell you. Although I'm quite disappointed you did not figure it out yourself. I always expected more from the son of a Space Jumper."

A Space Jumper? What was she talking about? "You're crazy," I said. "I'm a human."

"He does not need to know this," growled Sar Cyrillus.

"I want to know," Weegin said, who was now quite comfortable, watching the events unfold in front of him.

"A Space Jumper?" Max said.

"Quite handsome, too," Madame Lee added.

"I don't believe you," I said.

"That's impossible. JT's father died over one hundred years ago on the *Renaissance,*" Theodore said.

Madame Lee rolled her eyes and shook her head. "What are they teaching these children?"

"Madame Lee is an immortal," Weegin said.

"Thank you, Weegin, but not really."

"She's over twelve hundred Earth years old," he added.

Theodore started calculating. "Throw in some interstellar space jumping and the time dilation could make it possible. If the speed of light is 186,000 miles per second . . ." he mumbled.

"I like this one. He shows potential," Madame Lee said, stroking Theodore's chin with her long black fingernails. "Your father wanted to leave Orbis. He grew tired of our petty bickering and a life of exile. He chose a simpler life on another planet. Your rotting little planet, that is."

"If you're telling the truth, why would he come back, then?" I asked.

"Oh, I am telling the truth. Leaving the comfort and security of your own home is never easy. He believed that every person needed to make that journey to improve their station and fortify their character. But in order to leave the Trust, he accepted one more mission. A ridiculous mission. The details were on that drive," she said, motioning to the factory floor. "But I'm afraid it was a mission I did not want completed, and I'll do anything to get my way. Anything."

I just stared at her. What did she mean? Madame Lee only smiled.

"History shows us that space travel always brings its share of risks, but it wasn't easy when your ship was light-years away," Madame Lee said, reading my mind. "I only wish I had destroyed the whole thing now. I would have, too, had I known they'd brought a carton of human eggs on board. But with your father gone, there was no way his mission could be completed. Besides, we never would have had the chance to meet," she added.

"You killed my parents?" I said.

"And mine?" Theodore added.

"It was *you* who made the cryogenic sleepers fail?" Max said.

"Peons." Madame Lee's voice was full of scorn.

"Why did you kill them?" Theodore asked.

"His father forced my hand. I asked Quirin not to take the mission. I even begged him, which is very unbecoming for a Sinovian. The mission was foolish, nothing more than myths and rumors," Madame Lee said. "The universe will meet its fate, and nothing can stop it. But Quirin thought he knew better."

"You're wrong," I said. "My father's name was not Quirin. It was Sam. Sam Turnbull," I said. "And what did his mission have to do with you, anyway?"

Madame Lee shook her head and said, "So much of your mind is in the dark."

"I think Madame Lee had a thing for your father," Weegin said, taking great pleasure in piecing everything together.

"Never," I said. "He would never have had anything to do with someone like you."

"This is ridiculous," Sar Cyrillus said. "We do not have time for this."

"Is that why Johnny's a softwire?" Theodore asked.

"It's his destiny," Madame Lee said.

"I don't believe in destiny," I told her.

"What *you* believe is as important to me as those lives I destroyed. And if you don't do exactly as I say, I will add you, your friends, and your sister to that very unimportant list."

A hate grew in my belly such as I had never known. There was not a rational thought left inside my head. Any fear that I felt now disappeared. My mind was focused on vengeance and nothing else. I glared at Madame Lee. I would have my revenge.

She read my mind and simply laughed. "Please, child."

17

Madame Lee left the ugly Neewalker with Weegin. She gave him strict orders to kill Weegin if he attempted to contact anyone. Then she ordered everyone else out of Weegin's World. A transport, guarded by two more Neewalkers, waited for us in the exact same spot where we had said good night to Charlie.

Sar Cyrillus forced the remaining Neewalkers to sit in the back of the transport with Max, Theodore, and myself. The vehicle reeked of Neewalkers, a fishy stench mixed with grease and sweat that matured in such close quarters. Theodore held his nose as long as he could, but he eventually gave up.

"You guys really stink," Max said, but the Neewalkers did not respond. They simply stared at me. I could only assume the story of what I had done to the red-and-white-faced Neewalker had spread among their ranks. But they did not scare me. There was not a drop of fear in my body anymore. As far as I was concerned, I was dead anyway.

The trip took a very long time, and Max and Theodore kept dozing off, despite the putrid air. There was too much on my mind for sleep. First of all, where was Ketheria?

Whatever Madame Lee wanted me to do, I needed to secure Ketheria's safety first. I would do whatever she asked until I knew my sister was safe. Then I would get my revenge.

"Do you think she was telling the truth about your father?" Theodore was awake.

"I don't trust anything she says," I answered.

"Why would your father want to come back?"

"He's not my father," I said.

"Well, it might explain your abilities."

He did have a point. I had begun to assume that the prolonged spaceflight and my parents' science background had something to do with my being a softwire. It had never entered my mind that my father might be a Space Jumper. *Why isn't Ketheria a softwire, then?* Maybe there were no female Space Jumpers. So many questions bounced around in my head. And what about Ketheria? Who would have known she was a telepath! And why did that Quirin guy come back — and with all those humans?

My head was spinning. This was too much information for me to take in. I now knew how Theodore felt the day he uplinked too much at social studies class. But I needed to concentrate on the task at hand. I had to get Ketheria back. I focused every cell in my body on that task.

When the transport finally came to a stop, we were forced to wait with the Neewalkers until the doors were unlocked. What little air circulated within the moving vehicle now evaporated. When Sar Cyrillus finally opened the back of the transport, we jumped out and gasped in the fresh air.

Max tapped me on the shoulder. I was not

prepared for what I saw. I didn't know where we were on the ring, but Madame Lee was preparing for war right under the nose of the Keepers. And she prepared well. Thousands of Neewalkers were camped in fields below a spaceship that looked like it was cut from a single piece of vulcanized metal. We stared in amazement at the sight of Madame Lee's army.

"Look," Theodore said, pointing toward a large pond.

"They're like fish," Max said as one of the Neewalkers struggled toward the water without his stilts. Once in the water, his short, finned legs gave him more agility and speed than he ever demonstrated on land.

Sar Cyrillus marched us toward the sleek and sinister spaceship, stopping at a small camp below its belly.

"This is far enough," he said.

Madame Lee, who must have boarded the ship while we waited in the transport, now descended the craft on a lift. She smiled at us with an evil, knowing grin.

"Impressive, isn't it?"

"For a murderer," Max said.

"You earthlings love to label things, don't you?"

"Remember, she can read your mind," Theodore whispered to Max.

"That's right," Madame Lee said, and Max gave her a nasty look. "My, such spiteful thoughts for a young lady."

"Let's get this over with," I said.

"That's what I want to hear."

"Tell me what you want me to do." Madame Lee raised her eyebrows. I thought of anything but my plan. I did not want to give Madame Lee any more ammunition than she already had. I could see her trying to read my mind. It was a familiar look that I had seen often on Ketheria's face. How I didn't recognize it before, I'll never know.

Clear your mind, clear your mind.... But I had to think of something. The sweet taste of Ketheria's favorite treat — toonbas. That's what I thought about.

"Fine, have it your way," Madame Lee said. "Besides, do you know what those disgusting things are made from?"

"If I do what you want, I get Ketheria back, right?"

"Of course. I always keep my promises."

Max made a snorting noise.

"Then what do you want me to do?" I asked.

Madame Lee stood up and faced the thousands of Neewalkers below. "I *will* fulfill my destiny. The seed is within me! Now it is time we take what we need. What *I* need," she said. "And I need you to enter the central computer and destroy the Keepers' security controls before they commit you to their servitude. With this done, I will march on Magna."

"Forget it," Max said.

"Yeah, never," Theodore added.

"Fine, let's get started," I said.

"What!" Max and Theodore said together.

"You said it yourself, Max: Maybe it's the Keepers who are causing the computer malfunctions. Maybe she's the victim. Besides, the Keepers want me to live in there forever anyway. I'll be dead to everyone, so what do I care?"

"But she's a murderer, JT. You'll be helping someone who killed our parents."

"I never met my parents, did I?" I said.

"Because of her!" Max pointed at Madame Lee.

"I've made my choice," I told her.

"Very smart boy," Madame Lee said. "We will do great things together." Madame Lee ran her hand over my hair. I just stood there as Max and Theodore stared in disbelief.

"But you'll destroy Orbis 1," Max pleaded.

"I'm not very fond of this place anymore," I said.

"JT, she killed our parents."

I simply shrugged and turned to Madame Lee. Theodore and Max stared at each other as we walked away with Sar Cyrillus.

Toonbas, toonbas, toonbas, toonbas, toonbas . . .

The inside of Madame Lee's ship was nothing like the *Renaissance.* I did not see any controls or instruments. A solitary chair suggested that the ship could be piloted by a single passenger, despite the spacecraft's massive size. Madame Lee led me to something that resembled an O-dat.

I tried desperately not to think about what had just happened with Max and Theodore. I had a plan and I couldn't risk Madame Lee finding out. I sat at the O-dat and frowned.

"What's wrong?" Madame Lee asked me.

"This won't work."

"What do you mean?" she said.

"I can't access the central computer from here."

"Make it work," Sar Cyrillus demanded.

"I'll only be able to read files from it, then," I said. "I can only *push* when I'm near a main portal."

"Wait," Madame Lee said. She looked at me very carefully, trying to sniff out my lie. She whispered to Sar Cyrillus while I stared at the O-dat.

Toonbas, toonbas, toonbas, toonbas, toonbas . . .

"What do you mean by *push*?" she asked.

"It's how I get inside the computer. It's how I manipulate it."

She leaned in and threatened in the meanest tone, "If you're lying to me, you will never, ever, see your sister again."

"I'm not lying. I can try from here if you want. I don't know if it will work, but I'll give it a shot." I turned back to the console, hoping she bought it.

"Let him attempt it from here," Sar Cyrillus said.

"We don't have enough time if he fails. Come with us," she said to me.

As I exited the ship, the magnitude of her army unfolded in front of me. How had she gathered so many? Some Neewalkers drove strange single-wheeled craft instead of walking on stilts, and others drove large transports. I could only wonder how an army this large could go undetected on the ring.

"Much easier than you think, I'm afraid," Madame Lee said, reading my mind.

I looked up at her — *Toonbas, toonbas, toonbas, toonbas.*

Max and Theodore hadn't moved an inch from where we left them.

"What do you want me to do with them?" Sar Cyrillus said.

"Kill them," Madame Lee said without hesitation.

"Wait!" I shouted. "You can't kill them."

"Yeah," Theodore added.

"Why not?" she asked.

I looked at Max and Theodore before I turned to Madame Lee.

"Because they are my family, too. If you kill them, I won't help you. You might as well kill us all right here," I said. "It makes no difference to me without them."

Sar Cyrillus reached for his sword.

"If you don't get in that transport right now, I will kill your sister and force you to watch her die," Madame Lee growled at me, growing more and more impatient.

"You need me," I said. "You may not need them, but I do. There's no deal without them." I went and stood next to Max and Theodore. Sar Cyrillus gave me a steely look that told me this was not over.

"Kill them anyway," she said.

I stood between my friends and we took each other's hands. Sar Cyrillus drew his sword. The sharp blade flickered in the light.

"I will enjoy this," he said.

Theodore closed his eyes. "Good-bye, JT."

"Good-bye, Theodore," I said.

The Neewalker raised his sword over our heads.

I looked at Max. She squeezed my hand and smiled softly. We both closed our eyes.

"Wait! Argh, humans!" Madame Lee snorted. "Put them all in, then, if he needs them so badly." She stomped over to the transport.

"Next time I will not hesitate," Sar Cyrillus whispered, and he pushed us toward the vehicle.

The three of us sat in the back of the stinky transport by ourselves. Madame Lee rode with Sar Cyrillus up top.

"I thought we were goners," Theodore said.

"You didn't think I would leave you there, did you?" I said.

I looked at Max, but she was not warming up.

"I do not want to be any part of a plan that will destroy Orbis 1. I will not work for that monster," she said.

"You have a plan, don't you? You have no intentions of doing what she said, right?" Theodore asked, making me smile.

Max finally understood that there was a plan.

"A little slow there," I said.

We all laughed, despite what we knew was waiting for us.

"I'm going to get the little girl in the computer to help me."

The laughing stopped.

"You're kidding me, right?" Max said, dropping her head into her hands.

"The one you see in your dreams?"

Theodore wasn't excited by this plan, either. He lowered his head and stared at his feet.

"I couldn't tell you back there because I didn't want Madame Lee to listen to your thoughts."

"Don't worry, JT. Even if she did, I don't think she would have understood a word," Max said.

"I certainly don't," Theodore added.

"No, listen to me. She, this thing, the virus — I'm positive she's been causing the computer malfunctions. The Keepers and the Trading Council mistrust each other so much they can only point fingers at each other. While they bicker, Madame Lee is using the malfunctions to camouflage her plans to control Orbis. If I can get the virus on my side and get her to stop causing the malfunctions, then I can expose Madame Lee."

"I don't even know where to start, there are so many holes in that plan. Do you not remember that this virus tries to kill you every time you get close? Am I the only one who remembers this little detail? Even if you're right and you do stop the virus, how will that help you?" Max asked.

"She's got a point," Theodore said.
"Besides, you can't even talk to her."

"Ones and zeros," I said.

Max held her hands up. "What does that mean?"

"Remember Charlie? He talked about binary code, the ones and zeros that used to run the old computers."

"So what?"

"The virus *was* trying to talk to me. She wants to communicate with me. She left ones and zeros everywhere. First I thought it was the number ten, but that doesn't make sense. She only knows binary code."

"How is that going to help you?" Theodore asked.

"I don't know yet."

"Great!" Max threw her hands up again.

"Why wouldn't the computer just destroy the virus?" Theodore added.

"Because I think she's alive."

"What?" they both said.

"No, listen to me: The computer doesn't know what to do with a life force, not yet, anyway. It doesn't spit everything out, like people have been saying. Look at me. I feel the computer scanning me the moment I push in, but it always just lets me do my thing. It's the same way with the virus. I think that, despite what everyone says, the computer is not perfect. Maybe in time it will discover how to deal with the little girl, but right now it doesn't have a clue."

I knew I was right. If I could just find the virus, figure out how to talk to her, and then persuade her to help me, I could warn the Keepers and avert a war. It was simple, really. But Max and Theodore still looked uneasy.

"Do you remember when you were the only ones who believed me when I said I could talk to Mother?"

They both nodded.

"Well, you have to believe me now when I tell you this plan will work. I just know it."

No one said anything.

"Max?" I pleaded.

"Fine," she said. "But I'm not happy about this."

"Remember, clear your mind. Think about anything else. This is extremely important. We don't want Madame Lee to know," I reminded them.

"I hope you're right, JT," Max said.

"I am."

The transport came to an abrupt stop. Theodore toppled over and landed in a puddle of sludge.

"Ew!"

He was trying to wipe his hand off on the wall of the transport when the doors flew open.

"Let's go — quickly," Sar Cyrillus ordered.

This part of Orbis was unrecognizable to me. Seven white cylindrical structures, arranged in no particular pattern, towered above us. They stood at least three hundred meters tall. Atop each hung three layers of enormous sails that slowly spun around each structure. Some sails lay out flat, while others turned straight up or straight down. I could not even begin to guess what these structures were built for.

"We don't know, either," Madame Lee said, walking past me toward one of them. "But we've made good use of them."

Close off your thoughts! I reminded myself.

"I'm sure you have," Max said, her voice laced with sarcasm.

Theodore poked Max in the sides. "We're lucky to be alive. Can we try and stay that way?"

The interior of the structure provided no additional clues. Beautifully crafted hollow crystal globes of every color were nestled in the walls as if waiting for something. For some reason I felt relieved that these buildings did not belong to Madame Lee.

"They will," Madame Lee said.

Toonbas, toonbas, toonbas, toonbas, toonbas...

"Be careful what you think," Max whispered to me.

"I'm trying."

"Try harder," she said.

Deep in my mind, behind my thoughts of Ketheria's favorite sweets, I was trying to devise a plan. How would I make contact with the virus? What if the virus wouldn't stop? Max and Theodore kept glancing at me as if to see whether I had finally come up with something. I shrugged in response.

Madame Lee led us down one sterile corridor after another, each containing nothing but more crystal globes. The building was completely deserted. The only noise was the *clunk, whirl, clunk, zing* of the Neewalker's mechanical stilts. It was clouding my ability to think. I needed more time.

"You'll have all the time you need, but I don't think your sister does, so get to work," Madame Lee said.

She opened a door and said, "You'll find everything you need in here."

I filed into the room with my friends. Several O-dats were positioned around the room. Unlike the ones I was used to, these O-dats were attached to large computers. Max touched a few of the wires, admiring the work someone had done to put all of this in here.

"Thank you. It's much harder for me to monitor what people are doing on Orbis 1 than it is for our little softwire here."

"They should not have seen this," Sar Cyrillus said.

"You spy on people with this stuff?" Theodore asked.

"*Spying* is such a dirty word, don't you think? Let's say I use it to reach out to others, shall we?" Madame Lee said as Sar Cyrillus checked each machine. "I have no problem using these computers to distract everyone when I find it necessary."

"You *were* causing the computer malfunctions," Max said.

"What is this obsession with details?" she replied.

"But you didn't cause all of them?" I asked.

"It's only a computer, despite what the Keepers tell everyone. It makes mistakes," Madame Lee said. "Besides, your arrival was perfect timing. Citizens are so jumpy around softwires."

It was then that I realized that no one, not even Madame Lee or the Keepers, knew about the virus.

"And just in case you're trying to scheme up some foolish plan while attempting to block your mind with those childish candy treats —" Madame Lee flipped on a small O-dat in the corner.

"Ketheria!"

I ran to the screen. Ketheria was in some sort of holding cell. It resembled the one I was kept in when the Keepers were studying me.

"Just like the one you were in," Madame Lee said, and she tapped the screen. The image pulled back to reveal Ketheria in a single blue cell high above the ground in the Science and Research building. Almost all of the other cells were gone or hanging in disarray. I could see Ketheria look down and then start to scream when she saw the front wall of the cell blink on and off.

"If you don't do what I ask in — oh, say, this long" — Madame Lee motioned to Sar Cyrillus and he slapped a liquid-crystal timer on the wall next to the O-dat. The red liquid crystals began dripping into the empty reservoir below it — "then the floor of the containment cell that's holding her up right now will begin to blink off. You remember that effect, don't you?"

I remembered the ceiling to my blue cell blinking off and the slopcrawler falling through and the wall going out and my sleeper sliding down —

"Exactly," she said, reading my mind.

"How long is that?" Max said.

"Just make sure it's long enough," Madame Lee replied.

Madame Lee and the Neewalker went to the door.

"Where are you going?" I asked.

"I have an army to get ready. So many things to do." She cackled, and with that, the door closed behind her.

"The liquid crystal is moving pretty fast," Theodore said.

He was right. At this rate I had less than a diam — a lot less. I rushed to the computer terminal.

"Wait," Max said as she opened the door. "Why didn't they lock us in?"

"Where would we go?" Theodore asked. "We don't even know where we are."

"You watch him, Theodore. I'm going to get help."

"Be careful," I said. "Don't let anyone see you."

18

"Once I'm inside, I should still be able to hear you," I told Theodore. "Stay and watch the door. Warn me if Madame Lee comes back."

"JT?" Theodore looked very nervous.

"What?"

"Good luck."

"Thanks, but I hope I won't need it."

I pushed into the computer and felt the familiar rush of electrons across my face. I moved quickly along the network, looking for a portal out. There were more than fifty paths leading from Madame Lee's computer array. She was a busy alien. I picked a portal at random and shot through.

I commanded the computer to give me any information on my sister. As I traveled, several files came dashing forward. Files about her assignment to Weegin, reports to the Keepers and the Trading Council — all of them amounted to nothing more than paperwork. Not one of them mentioned Ketheria's imprisonment in the Science and Research building. I tried to access the building's files, but all I got was an error message.

I turned my thoughts to the virus and tried to imagine where the little girl might choose to hide. I called up a schematic of the computer's main structure and located the trash. She had been there once before; maybe I would find her there again.

Getting there was easy this time, but there was no sign of the virus.

Where is she?

Did I really believe I would just push into the computer and find her? *It happened before,* I reassured myself.

I shot through another network port, scanning every nook and cranny I could find, but she was nowhere.

I pulled out.

"What did you find?" Theodore asked, anxiously jumping up from the floor.

"Nothing. I can't find her."

"There's nothing in this building, either, just more and more computers," Max said, returning from her scouting mission. "I think Madame Lee's gonna put them online once you've broken down the central computer's defenses."

"Let's just get out of here and find the Keepers," Theodore said.

"It's too easy," Max said.

"Then let's do it," Theodore pleaded.

"She's right," I said. "Madame Lee wouldn't have left us here if we could just walk away."

I didn't know what to do next, and time was running out for Ketheria.

"Forget the virus, JT. Go to the Keepers. Warn them and then help Ketheria. Madame Lee has no idea what you can do," Max said.

I looked at the O-dat on the wall. Ketheria was stretched out on the floor. I could tell she was still crying. The crystal timer on the wall kept on dripping.

"Go," Max said, pointing to the screen.

"You're right." I sat down and pushed back into the computer.

Back through another network portal, I called up the schematic again and located the Keepers' grid. I pushed through as fast as I could, but it was far — a lot farther than I normally went. I could feel myself stretching very thin, and I was reminded of Theylor's warning: *Never get caught in the computer, Johnny. Your body will die.* Isn't that what they wanted, anyway? I had no choice right now. I kept pushing.

The portal I traveled along opened onto a large cache that exposed several entrances to the Keepers' mainframe.

Every single one of them was locked.

Not with a simple security device, either. Each portal was blocked with the security device that Theylor had shown me during our experiments.

That's why he wanted me to test it. To see if anyone could get through.

The Keepers were waiting for me — or someone else.

I studied the portals, but nothing Theylor had shown me had equipped me for this. I didn't have a clue, and time was running out for Ketheria. I pulled out.

Max and Theodore jumped up from the floor.

"It's no use. The Keepers must have prepared

for me. They studied my ability and built a device to keep me out," I said.

"It's obvious they were trying to keep someone out, but that doesn't mean it was you," Max said. "Besides, don't they want you to protect it?"

I glanced at the liquid clock next to the O-dat of Ketheria.

"Don't look at that," Theodore told me.

"I'm never going to be able to save her."

"Then save Orbis, JT," Max said quickly.

"What?"

Max moved next to my O-dat. "What if all of this is a ploy? A ploy to keep you busy while Madame Lee and the Neewalkers march on Magna? With you out of the way, it only makes it that much easier."

I didn't buy it. "I'm not that much of a threat," I argued.

"But a threat all the same," Max said.

I looked back at Ketheria.

"Maybe this is what you're supposed to do," Max said.

"What is?"

Max said, "Maybe this is why you came halfway across the galaxy — for this very moment. To save Orbis. It might not be what you expected, but we need you right now. Everyone needs you. Don't let Madame Lee win. That's your purpose. That's what you must do."

"She's right, Johnny. You've got to stop them."

"But how?"

"Warn them. Warn anybody. Overload the system. Use it," he said quickly, and Max nudged me toward the O-dat.

"Okay. I'll do everything I can," I said.

"I'll keep searching," Max said.

"What should I do?" Theodore said.

"You stay and guard the door. Don't let anyone in — except me, of course," Max said.

"How will I do that?"

"Just think of something," Max said, and she left once more. I pushed back into the computer. Theodore sat against the wall and watched me.

How was I going to send a message? I'd never done that before. I thought of a blank file and then tried to think about what I wanted to say.

Beware: Neewalkers are marching on Magna. Simple — probably not very effective. *Hi, my name is Johnny Turnbull. You don't know me, but I've been told that Madame Lee is about to attack Magna with an army of Neewalkers.* Equally ineffective, I decided.

I pushed farther into the computer, with no particular direction. I had no idea what to do. At that moment I would have traded anything to buy more time.

"Charlie!" I said out loud. He would believe me.

I accessed the computer grid to locate the Center for Impartial Judgment and Fair Dealing. On the way, I accessed every file containing the name Charlie. Thousands came up in front of me. What was Charlie's last name? Howards? Howen? Nor —

Norton!

Nothing. There was no Charlie Norton anywhere in the computer system. *How can that be? I've got to find him.* I accessed the central computer for the Earth News Café.

The grid maneuvered in front of me and I saw the portals for each electronic menu at every table. I accessed them all at once.

Charlie,
It's Johnny. I know this sounds crazy, but I'm inside the central computer at this very moment. Madame Lee has us locked up and she's marching on Magna with an army of Neewalkers. Please believe me. They are holding Ketheria in a broken cell at the Science and Research building. They have threatened to kill her if I don't help them. Please help. Tell everyone.
Your friend,
Johnny Turnbull

I closed the file and hoped like mad it would work. Now what? I didn't have to look far to know what to do next.

Directly in front of me, bound against her wishes to a silicon chip, was the little girl I so desperately wanted to find. The virus struggled frantically to free herself from a ruthless stream of code that entangled her legs and right arm. It looked as if the central computer had finally managed to nab the errant virus and had begun systematically removing pieces of her program. She was snatching them away with her free hand and stuffing them into her mouth. She wasn't fast enough, though, and small chunks of code were being deposited along the light paths and moving toward the trash. The virus, which once looked so powerful, was crying like the little girl I first thought she was.

She saw me as I moved toward her, and she recognized me at once. The look on her face this time, however, was one of pure terror. The central computer was slowly destroying her.

"What can I do to help?" I asked her, but she only looked at me with a puzzled expression. The closer I got, the more clearly I could see the colored code beneath her transparent skin. It was nothing like the computer code I was used to. "Let me help you," I said, only slower and louder, as if this would make a difference. She still couldn't understand anything I was saying.

I pushed at the stream of code that tied her right arm. She struggled to pull away from me even though it was impossible. "It's okay. I just want to help." But it was no use. The code would not move, and the computer was slowly taking more and more pieces away from her. She could only swallow back so much of it.

The little girl opened her mouth as if to cry, but let out a sound that almost made me flee back to Theodore and Max. Her piercing scream penetrated the core of my brain. It was the sound I had heard when the *Renaissance* was docking. The same sound as when the sorting bays were being destroyed. I wanted to tell her to stop crying, but how could I communicate with her? I could not speak binary code. And that's when it dawned on me.

The translation codec.

No one could understand her, and she obviously could not understand me, because of her language — or whatever you called the noise she made. The central computer never translated it. Maybe she spoke a language that Orbis had never encountered in the last ninety thousand years. It was possible. That must be it.

I accessed the computer for the translation codec. In an instant, the file with the small program was right in front of me.

"Use this program," I told her, moving the program toward her head. "Then I'll be able to und —"

The virus just stared at me and continued to scream. She didn't understand a word I was saying.

"Please stop that noise."

How was I going to get her to use the program? Would she even be able to use it? *This is a dumb idea,* I thought. I needed to get to Ketheria.

"I'm sorry," I said to the little girl, who took the program with her free hand and began to eat it. "It's not food. I wish I could give you something."

The little girl did not seem to care. She gave herself up to the central computer and stopped fighting. I headed back to Theodore.

"Help me."

I whipped around. The virus had spoken to me.

"Help me," the little girl repeated.

"Do you understand what I'm saying?" I asked her.

The little girl's eyes widened at the sound of my words.

"How do you speak my words? No one in two million years has spoken my words." The little girl winced as the computer removed another chunk of code.

"Listen to me. The computer thinks you are a virus. It's trying to destroy you. It wants to eliminate your code."

"Why?" the virus asked, acting more like a little girl than ever.

"You've done some damage while you've been inside the central computer."

The virus looked at me the same way Ketheria looks at me when I scold her.

"I'm sorry, I was only looking to be whole again. I have so many memories of flesh."

"Can you copy yourself?"

"It's not in our ability. That can only be performed by the High Memory."

"There are more of you?" I asked her, worried about the answer.

"Not here. Very, very far away, on the edge of this universe," she said, and I sensed in her voice the longing to be home. "I escaped. I ran away."

"But can one of these High Memory guys copy you?"

"I'm too far from one. I've been traveling for billions of light-years." The virus began to cry.

I saw a real tear on the transparent skin that covered the yellow and magenta computer code now flowing through her body.

I pushed into the virus's code. The alien programming was unlike anything I'd ever seen. The complexity of its codecs and architecture was beyond my comprehension. I felt, however, that I was truly inside a living being.

I snapped out of the virus.

"You are a High Memory!" the little girl said in a very excited manner. "Please do not punish me for the things I did to you. I did not know. I thought you were trying to destroy me."

"Hold on. Hold on there, I'm not a . . . a . . . Higher Memory guy — thing."

"You have to be. Only a High Memory would be able to do what you just did. You must copy me, and quickly."

"I don't know how, you're so . . . complex —"

"Please, hurry!"

Hurry was definitely something I had to do. Time was running out for Ketheria, too. If only Max were here. She would know how to do this. I thought about the mirror copy Max made for me from the *Renaissance*'s drive. I accessed an empty file, created a new directory, placed it outside my personal files, and . . . and then what? How was I going to get her onto another file? I had no idea what to do next.

"I'm sorry. I don't know how," I said, looking back at the virus, but she did not respond.

Instead she began to glow. The code under her skin moved so fast I could no longer make it out. Then the little girl's programming lifted from her body and began writing to the mirror directory I had created next to her. The light intensified, filling the passageway where she was bound to the hardware as the code began transferring faster and faster.

It was beautiful watching the new virus — the new alien, that is — taking form. Magenta streams of the little girl's code swirled around the mirror directory before finding their rightful place. The central computer began adding more streams of its own code to hold her old form down, but it was no use now. The new destination folder began to take shape. I could begin to see the outline of the little girl.

I watched as the master copy went limp. The central computer quickly began dismantling what was left of the old virus as the little girl opened her new eyes.

"You *are* a High Memory," she said thickly as the static from the electron surge faded.

"Whatever you say," I replied. "But right now I need your help."

"Anything." The little girl was smiling, looking at her newly formed arms.

"Do you have a name?" I asked her.

"No one has spoken my name in so very long.

The Elders once called me Vairocina."

"Hello, Vairocina. My name is Johnny Turnbull; my friends call me JT. It's a pleasure to finally meet you."

"Hello, Johnny Turnbull," she said, closing her eyes and holding her hands in a very formal fashion.

"Who are you? What are you doing in the computer?"

"I heard about the magical Rings of Orbis many, many light-years ago, when I journeyed in the brain computer of a galaxy merchant. I had been without a body so long, I hoped I would find one here. It was foolish to think I could be whole again."

"Again?"

"I was once of flesh, but after my accident, the Elders uploaded my consciousness to our planet's digital neural society. It was terrible, so I ran away."

"I wish I could do the same," I told her.

"But why? You are a High Memory. You can do whatever you please."

"Uh . . . yeah . . . well, there's a lot more to it than that, but do you remember the new barriers created for the network portals?"

"Silly little tricks." She glanced at where her body once lay.

"I can't get through them. You have to show me."

"Anything you like, High Memory. Follow me."

The little girl zipped in and out of the central computer with ease. It was her playground. There wasn't an obstacle she couldn't get through. By the time we reached the Keepers' domain, I knew I had traveled too far. I felt very weak, very thin. I was stretching beyond the limits of my abilities. Bands of color circled my head, and everything was washed in a gray static. I slowed to a stop, but Vairocina went straight through the portal.

"Wait." But she was gone.

I attempted to follow her, but I might as well have tried to walk through the hull of a spaceship. I could not get through.

"Vairocina!" I shouted, but no one answered.

"How do you —"

And then every portal to the Keepers' domain opened at once. Vairocina stood in the middle opening.

"Come this way," she said, smiling.

"You'll have to show me how to do that."

"Shall I do that now, my Cynosure?"

"Cynosure? What's that? I'm JT."

"But you are a High Memory. It's not proper that I call you by your common name."

"I'm not Higher — oh, just forget it. Listen, Madame Lee wants to use these portals to attack Orbis 1. We must warn my friends and warn the Keepers."

"Follow me," she said.

Inside the portals, the Keepers' computer seemed far more crowded with files and hardware. This slowed us down as we pushed deeper into the Keepers' domain.

"We must be in Magna," I said.

"This is where the two-headed people live," Vairocina said. "They do not like me."

"That's because they think you are trying to destroy their home."

Vairocina had a puzzled look on her face. "I am not trying to destroy their home."

"Then why do you break things from inside the computer, like Weegin's World? You destroyed his giant sorting factory."

Vairocina got angry. "I did not destroy that. It was attacking me. I was visiting your sleeping devices when I came upon the attack. I did everything to stop it, but you got in the way. It would have been destroyed if I hadn't arrived."

"Okay, you don't have to get so upset."

I guessed the destruction at Weegin's World was Madame Lee's doing. Not only did it distract everyone on Orbis, but it also enabled her to buy off Weegin and get closer to me.

"Where I am from, it is insulting to accuse someone of something they didn't do," Vairocina said, looking dejected.

"It's supposed to be like that where I'm from, too. I'm sorry, but don't get too upset, because you're getting blamed for a lot of things right now."

We both floated to a clearing inside the computer. I looked up and saw a large opening. I could see my reflection. I floated up and saw familiar symbols forming in the dark void, only they appeared backward. I pressed myself close against the transparent barrier high above the computer floor.

"I know where this is," I said to Vairocina. I could see Keepers. Drapling stood next to the dark pool, glancing at the surface. He shouted with both heads at the other Keepers.

"Hey! Help! In here!" I pounded against the surface.

"They can't hear you," Vairocina said.

"We have to warn them; then I can rescue my sister," I told her.

"You have a sister? Here?"

"Yes, her name is Ketheria. You kind of remind me of her. They have her locked up in the Science and Research building."

"I had a brother once — and a mother and a father. But that was when I had a physical form. When I was of flesh." Vairocina held her hands up, looking at the computer code running through her veins. I saw the sadness on her face. "I miss them very much, but that was a long, long time ago."

"I'm sorry, Vairocina. I miss my sister, too, and if I don't get to her, they are going to let her die."

"What do we do? I must help."

I stared at the dark pool.

"Do you want me to work the interface?" Vairocina asked, pointing to the pool.

"What do you mean?"

"The black water. It is similar to the screens everyone uses. I have watched you use them."

"You've watched me?"

Vairocina dropped her head.

"I am sorry, High Memory. Please do not be angry."

"Stop it. I'm not a High Memory. I'm a kid, just like you . . . well, I think," I said, looking up at the Keepers' pool. "If that's an interface, then we can use it."

Vairocina lifted her head, smiling. "Let me do it for you."

"Fine, the translation codec I gave you should let you speak with any alien race on Orbis —"

"And thank you for that," she interrupted. "It has been so long since I have conversed with another being. Such a simple gift, for which I can never repay you."

"Yeah, okay. But wait — the symbols in that pool do not translate. The Keepers never added that language to the translation codec on the central computer. They must have some sort of secret language hidden behind one of their barriers. You must find that language and assimilate with the central computer. I don't think I can go any farther. Can you do that?"

"Absolutely. I've been living inside computers for millions of years. Nothing gets in my way now," she said, full of pride, and with that, Vairocina vanished.

"Wait —" But she was gone again. "Vairocina, where are you?" I panicked.

"I can still hear you," Vairocina said in the same manner Mother would speak to me on the

Renaissance. It felt reassuring, in some weird way.

"Where did you go?"

"I'm accessing the archives for a translation. I only wish I knew about this earlier."

"You never asked."

Vairocina was back. "I have many more questions."

But they would have to wait.

"Watch out!" she screamed.

The moment Vairocina opened the portals, six monstrous programs stormed the main cache leading to the Keepers' mainframe.

"She must have been monitoring the portals!" I shouted.

The programs looked like machines, something used to tear up the ground. They lashed out at anything within their reach and quickly destroyed the walls of the main cache.

"Vairocina! Did you close the portals behind us?"

"I did not. I'm sorry."

"Warn the Keepers that an army is about to march on Magna. Hurry, please!"

Vairocina instantly disappeared as one of Madame Lee's digital soldiers fired a stream of electrons at her.

"Vairocina!"

"Is that what you were hiding behind your silly little thoughts?" Madame Lee said. A seventh and even larger program entered the portal. A life-size image of Madame Lee's head was positioned in the middle. Static electricity sparkled around the opening that held her head. I only hoped Vairocina had made it out.

"How did you get in here?" I said.

"Technology, my peon. You don't feel so special now, do you? I'll have an army of these creatures in here before the cycle is done. And then I can control everything from here. Destroy it all!" she screamed, and the sound of her voice tore through my brain like a rocket.

The programs drew energy from the central computer, directing the electrical flow to exact powerful strikes against the data fields. The resulting shock waves rolled over me, twisting my reality and striking up a firestorm of electricity.

"Stop!" I screamed, but Madame Lee only laughed.

I pushed into the destructive programs, but their codes changed with every attempt I made to breach their security. I pulled out of the demon program. There was nothing I could do but watch Madame Lee's army of data soldiers pulverize the central computer.

"I said everything!" she screamed at them as one of her demonic foot soldiers turned on me.

I felt the program latch onto my computer form. Its electrical claws wrapped around my face and drained out all the energy I had left. I instinctively tried to pull out of the central computer, but the program would not let go. It had me. My mind's eye flickered between the images of destruction and blue static.

    With one jerk, Madame Lee's monster ripped my essence from my body. My mind flashed bright white as ice-blue energy currents filled my veins and sent a burst of silvery flame charging through my bones and out through my fingertips. Static electricity crackled across my new form. I was completely inside the computer, just like Vairocina, but I knew that I was also still in my old body, caught between two realities. From deep inside my head, I felt my physical form slide off the chair back in the room with Theodore.

    "JT!" I heard Theodore screaming. "JT, what's wrong! Wake up!"

    Theodore shook my body, but I could not respond. I could hear and see him, but I was unable to move. I felt as if I were looking up at him from the bottom of a very deep well. Theodore ran to the door.

    "Max! Max! Come quick. JT is hurt." I didn't hear anything for a while after that. He must have left to find Max.

    The break from my physical form, although painful at first, left me bursting with the energy of the entire central computer. I steadied myself using my new limbs. Madame Lee's demonic programs were no match for me now. Manipulating them was as easy as tossing trash from Weegin's conveyor belts. I no longer pushed into anything. I was in everything. My mind reached out to a billion data points at once. I sucked knowledge from every source on Orbis and from every corner of the central computer. Dismantling each program would be as easy as thinking about it. A stream of fiery electrons shot from my hands as Madame Lee's demons scrambled for cover. The explosions left nothing but pieces of code floating in the air.

"Stupid little tricks," Madame Lee said as I turned on her. She released a fireball of electricity that sprang high above me and thundered down on my new form. To her horror, I simply absorbed the energy.

"That's it?" I said, and reached in and grabbed her face with my right hand.

"Don't!" she cried. A rush of electricity shot up my arm as I ripped Madame Lee from her program. She screamed in pain as the space around her crackled and sparked. I threw her form to the ground, where the central computer immediately began to dismantle the essence of Madame Lee, sending chunks of code to the trash.

"You can't do this!" she screamed, almost begging.

"Yes, I can," I said. As I watched Madame Lee thrash about, now under the control of the central computer, I felt a distant sensation of my physical form being moved. Caught in two places, I could at once see three scavenger robots encasing my real body inside a glass and metal disposal crate. The part of me that was still in that body could vaguely see them building the coffin around me. As Theodore returned to the room, I screamed from inside the computer that I was still alive, but no one could hear me.

"Stop!" Theodore screamed, too, but the drones would not let up.

Theodore kicked one of the robots, but it only paused momentarily before continuing. Theodore could only stand and watch as they welded a coffin around me.

He threw his arms around the closest drone and pulled it away from my lifeless form. There was nothing I could do. Inside the computer, I retraced my steps as the drone zapped Theodore with an electrical charge. He fell to the ground and then scrambled to the door.

"Max! Max!" I heard him shouting.

"The sails on the building have begun to turn. What's happening?" she said.

I could still hear her running down the hallway. My senses were alert, but they were fading — fading fast.

"They've got Johnny. I can't stop them."

"Who's got Johnny? What do you mean?" Max pushed past Theodore to see the drones completely entomb my body inside the glass and metal coffin.

"Stop!" she screamed, but the drones were no more responsive to her than to Theodore.

"Look, the globes on the walls are filling," Theodore shouted.

Images mixed with blue static filled my mind's eye. The drones pushed my coffin, which hovered a meter above the ground, toward the door. I could see Max through the glass as she put her weight against the coffin.

"Forget them — help me push it back," she yelled, but the drone zapped her before Theodore could react.

"Ow!"

The drones pushed me past my friends. Max scrambled to her feet and banged her fists against the glass. Theodore jumped on top of the glass tomb, and two robots zapped him at the same time. He fell to the floor. Max stared at Theodore's unconscious body.

"JT! JT! Wake up!" she screamed, but I could do nothing. I raced through the computer, hoping I could get to my body at the connection point. I needed to find a way back — now.

Max frantically tried everything she could to get the robots to stop, but nothing worked. As she searched for something to distract them with, I heard a hissing noise. Blue gas began to fill my tomb. Max screamed as the gas crept along my body.

Without thinking, she grabbed the closest robot and lifted it above her head. The robot zapped her several times, but she would not stop. She brought the robot crashing down on the glass coffin, shattering the top and destroying the robot.

The coffin fell to the floor while red flashing lights blinked from the two remaining robots. Max kicked one and they both scrambled away.

"I should have done that earlier," I heard her

say as she pulled my body from the debris.

Max slapped me on the face several times.

"Johnny! Johnny!"

"Is he all right?" Theodore, still a little groggy, came around the corner.

"I don't know. Help me get him back to the O-dat."

They struggled down the hallway and set me inside the room. It was very hard to see them now. I slipped farther down the well.

"Johnny!" Max slapped me very hard.

I could no longer sense my own flesh as a brilliant shard of golden lightning shut down my brain.

19

The bright white opening at the end of the well came rushing toward me, only to fade away again and again. As it came close once more, I lunged my entire essence at the light, knowing it was my only salvation.

Reboot. My eyes flickered open, and I gasped real air into my lungs. My head throbbed as I focused on the fixture in front of me.

"You have been doing that quite a few times, I am afraid."

"Theylor?"

"It is good to have you back," he said.

"But how . . . I . . ."

"Humans are a very strange species. Full of surprises, I must say. You showed great resilience. The cosmic energies in the building Madame Lee kept you in were unusually high."

"Ketheria? Where's Ketheria? I have to get . . ." I said, struggling to orient myself.

"Ketheria is fine. Relax, everyone is safe now, thanks to you."

"Madame Lee? The war? What happened?"

"Madame Lee's ship is gone. She has fled Orbis."

"But I killed her," I said.

"You may have done just that," he said. "Your message to Drapling took some time to understand,

I'm afraid, but your friend — I believe his name is Charlie — was smart enough to believe you."

"So it worked?"

"You should have come to us much sooner. We were monitoring Madame Lee's army for some time. Neewalkers do not come cheap, I am afraid."

"Sar Cyrillus?"

"With the help of Torlee. They were friends at one time. We did not know how Madame Lee would strike our defenses. We should have suspected she might try to use you. That is the same reason we needed you inside the central computer."

"I forgot about that. Do I still have to go? Can I say good-bye first?"

"Do not worry about that anymore. We have Vairocina now. Once again, thanks to you."

"Vairocina?"

"She was instrumental to us in destroying anything Madame Lee put in the computer. She will be a valuable asset to Orbis as long as you remain here with us. She has grown very fond of you."

"So I don't have to live in the computer?"

Theylor shook both of his heads. What a relief that was.

"How did you learn to communicate with Vairocina?" Theylor asked.

"After Charlie mentioned the ones and zeros, I realized she was trying to communicate with me the only way she knew how. I knew she was just code, in a manner of speaking, but still a living being all the same. She must have come to Orbis 1 in such a manner that she never received the translation codec."

"True. No one from her species has ever traveled the wormhole. Vairocina comes from a solar system at the very edge of the universe. Her people are a very old species of immortals. Through the millennia they rid their system of disease, war, famine — anything that would shorten their life cycle. When they were tired of their physical form but still wished to be in contact with their loved ones, they simply uplinked their consciousness and personality to a digital community. Very old and wise, this virtual community provided wisdom and guidance for every new generation."

"But Vairocina looks so young. How did she get in there?"

"When she was six years old, her physical form was damaged beyond repair in an accident. Her parents begged the Elders to uplink their daughter's consciousness so they could still communicate with her. They loved her very much. Never had such a young consciousness been placed in the community. She rebelled. She ran away. Vairocina jumped across the galaxies inside any device she could, anything she could store her consciousness in, as she searched for a new body. She ended up here in the belief that Orbis, with its riches, was a magical place."

"She will never have a physical form again, will she?" I asked.

"I am afraid not, but now she has a purpose. A

purpose on Orbis."

"One I am very excited about, too," Vairocina said.

"Vairocina?"

"Hello, Johnny."

"I can hear her in my head," I told Theylor. "Just like Mother."

He stood up. "Johnny, greatness has been thrust upon you, and you have performed with a dedication and a maturity that is a tribute to your species. I know you may not like the role you have been given, but sometimes it is not up to us to choose. Sometimes our purpose is shown to us, as it was with you. You have saved Orbis, and everyone is grateful for it. I am very interested to see the role of humans in our future. You will always have my admiration, Johnny. Now, please rest. Vairocina, if you can hear me, let Johnny rest now."

"I'm afraid he cannot hear me, JT, but you will not have time to rest. You have more visitors."

Just as Vairocina spoke, Ketheria, Max, and Theodore entered my recovery room.

"Guys!"

"I thought we lost you," Max said, and smiled.

"It's good to see you, Johnny," Theodore said.

"Thanks to you two," I told them.

My friends surrounded my bed. My sister stood next to me. Theylor rubbed his hand on Ketheria's head. "She's been through quite a lot," he said. "You might find your sister a little different."

"I'm glad you're safe," I told Ketheria.

She smiled and moved toward me. Max's eyes flashed with an excitement I didn't understand.

"What?" I said.

And then I heard something I never thought I would.

My sister squeezed my hand and opened her mouth. "I knew you would come back," she said.

JT's advenures continue in....

On Orbis 2, JT discovers that he alone can communicate with an amazing race of intelligent aquatic aliens -- and that they desperately need his help to escape a life of enslavement.

Turn the page for an excerpt...

"Here it comes!" Theodore Malone shouted.

"But we're not ready yet!" I yelled back, scoping the sorting bay for any sign of *it*. I snatched the hand laser off the floor and hid it inside my vest.

"Give me that," Maxine Bennett protested, and took the tool from me. She pointed it at the scavenger-bot now dissected on the metal floor in front of us. "This is the last one. If that thing gets its paws on this before we fix it, who's gonna clean this place up? Not me," she said. "I plan to do more on this ring than just pick up after Switzer."

I did too. I just hadn't figured what that was yet. I strained my neck to see past the huge cranes rooted on the inner dome at the center of Weegin's World. There was no sign of *it*.

"Fine, Max. Then you keep working, and I'll find some way to block the lift," I said, standing up and tearing back toward the other kids.

"Better hurry, JT," Theodore said from across the sorting-bay floor and to my far right.

"You could help," I told him, but Theodore shook his head. He was safely out of the way, perched atop one of the electric-blue sorting belts. The belts were placed every meter or so inside the curved factory. Theodore waved me over to join him on the gaseous device, but I needed to make it to the second-floor lift, located between him and the last belt.

Our roommate, Randall Switzer, was dozing on that farthest belt. I could see a portable O-dat clutched in his oversize paw. It was a weak attempt to prove his intelligence, but I knew the lazy malf only wanted to nap.

I heard the lift squawk into action. Theodore stood up on the belt. "It's on the lift! Forget about the bot, JT — just run!"

I froze. From where I stood, I couldn't see the lift, but I could definitely hear what was on it.

"Work! Work! Now work!" *it* screamed over the machine's metallic hum like a distress beacon.

"It's getting off the lift — now," another kid said.

I turned back toward Max. "Leave it," I shouted at her.

I took my chances and charged toward Theodore.

I hadn't even broken stride when my feet were knocked out from under me. Before I hit the floor, a heavy, clawed foot (the worst kind) thumped against the lower part of my vest, knocking the wind out of me.

"I see you with tools. Where you get tools?" *it* screamed at me.

"I'm fixing the scavenger-bot," I shouted back. "You broke them all!" But I knew speaking to him was useless. The bald little beast just tilted his head whenever I spoke, as if amazed I could make sounds with my mouth. It was worse than trying to reason with Switzer.

"My tools!" he said, and pushed down on my chest.

When I was first assigned to Weegin, almost one complete rotation ago, my Guarantor always cradled a yellowed larva in his thick, three-fingered hands. He nursed that puffy thing phase after phase, and I never once bothered to ask him what it was. No one did. Weegin answered most questions with a twist of your nose or your ear, or even a painful yank on your hair. If he had wanted me to know what it was, he would have told me. But the mystery was gone now. Two phases ago, right after I fought the Belaran, Madame Lee, inside the central computer, that puffy lump of flesh hatched into the little monster that stood over me as I gasped for air.

"Who gave knudnik my tools?" he demanded, and lifted his disgusting foot off my chest.

Previous confrontations with Weegin's offspring taught me to give up early since he never understood a word I said anyway. I simply curled up on the floor, clutched my stomach, and waited for the oxygen to find its way into my lungs. Looking satisfied with my condition, the undersize monster set his beady eyes on Switzer.

The alien was not exactly a miniature version of Weegin, as you might expect. His hands were far more muscular, and his legs appeared thicker and stronger than they should for a Choi from Krig. The bald protégé stalked the corridors of Weegin's World with his lower jaw thrust absurdly forward, the result of a severe underbite. A row of pointed teeth curled up and over his top lip as he marched around barking orders at everyone. Somehow this pink little maggot thought he was in charge.

He ran straight at Switzer and slammed the operation button next to his head. The sorting belts hissed into motion.

"Work. You. Big thing. Work now!" he yelled, and stood guard so no one could get at the controls.

Theodore had jumped to the floor. Switzer, however, remained soundly asleep. Even the clatter of the awakened cranes did not stir him.

"Maybe he's deaf *and* dumb?" Theodore said.

"Switzer!" Max shouted, but he did not move. Switzer kept right on sleeping as the blue mist holding him up headed for the chute. The chute was a hole in the wall that led to a furnace burning deep beneath Weegin's World. It was a drop Switzer would not survive. Max and another kid tried to get to Switzer, but Weegin's hatchling snapped his large, protruding snout at anyone who moved.

I pulled myself off the ground. "Distract that thing," I told Max, and she chucked a wrench at him. The alien turned on his heels and stomped straight toward her, his lengthy claws clacking on the metal floor.

"Tools are expensive!" he screamed.

I stuck my hand in the greenish-gray radiation gel used to protect our skin when there was junk to sort. I slid over to Switzer and reached my hand under his nose. The ghastly smell — rotten meat mixed with crusty socks and a touch of recycled toilet water — did the job. Switzer wrenched his head away and fell to the floor as Weegin dashed out from his glass bunker. I ran to an O-dat at the other side of the bay and accessed the local computer network with my softwire. I shut the cranes down instantly.

"Is it here? Speak. Is it here yet?" Joca Krig Weegin shouted from the second-floor balcony that jutted out over the sorting-bay floor. He hoisted his knobby body onto the railing and canvassed each one of us with his bloodshot eyes.

"Is what here, Weegin?" said a voice from the tall glass doorway.

I spun around to see the Keeper, Theylor. His purple velvety robes swept the floor as he entered Weegin's World.

"You're not welcome here!" Weegin screamed at the regal alien, raining spit on anyone below him. "They're mine. Every last one of them!" With that he turned and scrambled back into his office.

I saw Theylor's left head frown while his right head turned to all of us and said, "Hello. I hope everyone is fine?"

"We're a little bored," I said.

"No, *really* bored," Switzer added.

Switzer was right. There was nothing to do at Weegin's anymore. Our Guarantor's junk business was in shambles ever since his dealings with the disgraced Trading Council member, Madame Lee, had failed. Most cycles, I simply roamed around the complex while Weegin barricaded himself in his office. It was nowhere near the life I had imagined for Ketheria and myself before we had arrived on the Rings of Orbis.

"Hello? Hey! I need a little help here, anyone?" Max said, jumping from side to side using an even larger wrench to swipe at Weegin's offspring.

"Weegin hasn't even named that thing," Theodore said.

"His name is Nugget," said my sister, Ketheria, as she entered the sorting bay. She noticed Theylor immediately. "Hi, Theylor."

"Hello, Ketheria," he replied.

"Come here, Nugget," Ketheria said, and the creature immediately stopped harassing Max and marched over to Ketheria, sticking his chin out and up. For some reason he never bothered my little sister. Ketheria tickled him under his chin while he reached up and played with her light brown hair.

"Ooh, ooh," the alien moaned.

"Freak," Switzer said, sneering.

"Which one?" Dalton Billings said, and Max shot Switzer's friend a steely look.

"Why does she like that thing?" Switzer asked.

"Jealous?" Max teased him.

Switzer snarled at her but caught Theodore grinning. Theodore was easier prey for him than Max, and he moved toward my friend, fists raised. I stepped forward, too.

Nugget saw this and sprang to his feet, charging at us with his ridiculous lower jaw smacking against his upper lip.

"Work. Now. More work!"

"There is no work, you little rat," Dalton shouted at Nugget as he stomped past.

"He doesn't understand anything we tell him, Theylor," Max said.

As Nugget got close, Theylor raised his long right hand, and the alien was frozen in midstride. I could see a soft, warm glow from a bronze device wrapped around Theylor's arm. I'd seen him silence someone before, when we first arrived on the ring, but I'd never noticed that gadget before.

"*Thank* you," Max exclaimed.

"This may help," he said, and made a sweeping motion with his slender arm.

The blue translucent skin on his fingers peeked out from underneath his velvet robe as he pointed to an R5 that now entered Weegin's World. "Right there will be fine," he told the robot.

I hadn't seen an R5 since we first arrived on Orbis 1. The robot was used to implant neural ports behind everyone's left ear allowing them to link up with the central computer. Everyone but me, that is. I don't need a neural port. I am a softwire — a leap in human evolution that allows me to interact with any computer using only my mind. Some of the other kids, especially Max, think my ability is really golden, but I find it just makes most Orbisians very nervous. The Citizens think their precious computer is some kind of all-knowing, sentient being. It doesn't make them very happy knowing I can get inside it whenever I want.

"Who's that for?" Theodore asked.

"Who do you think, split-screen?" Switzer said, rolling his eyes and snickering with Dalton.

Ketheria stepped forward and said, "That's for Nugget."

"You are correct," Theylor told her.

"But why didn't Weegin take him to get this done earlier?" I asked.

"Yeah, it would have made life around here a lot easier," another girl said, frowning.

Theylor looked up toward Weegin's office. "It seems your Guarantor has been avoiding contact with us for quite some time."

I looked up and saw a mound of unanswered messenger drones stacked outside Weegin's office. They waited patiently to uplink the screen scrolls they carried with Weegin's neural implant, if he ever let them.

"What are they for?" I asked.

"First we must deal with . . ." Theylor began.

"Nugget. His name is Nugget," Ketheria reminded him.

Theylor looked at my sister and smiled. He placed his long, slender hand on her head without touching the strip of metal now physically attached to her skull. When Madame Lee exposed Ketheria's telepathy, Keeper decree required that she be fixed with a prosthetic to diminish her abilities. Ketheria didn't seem bothered by it, though, and her hair had grown back nicely, almost covering the sculpted metal that banded her head. My sister said she even liked the large amber crystal placed in the metal over her forehead. I asked her once if it hurt. She just shrugged and said, "Not anymore."

"How are you, Ketheria?" Theylor asked.

"I'm fine."

"I'm glad," the Keeper replied. "I am also glad Nugget has a friend."

"He's different from his father, isn't he? Weegin is a Choi, but Nugget is a Choisil," she said.

"I am afraid you are right," Theylor said. "It will be hard for Weegin to accept Nugget. But he has you now, Ketheria."

"Yes, he does," she replied.

I looked at Nugget, frozen in the middle of the sorting-bay floor, and I actually felt sorry for him, even though I didn't know what Ketheria was talking about.

"Can you unfreeze him?" Ketheria asked.

"Certainly."

Theylor raised his hand again, and the startled Nugget shot off across the bay.

"Enough with the reunion — let's implant the little bugger!" Switzer cried, scanning the room for Nugget.

Switzer had hated the implanting procedure more than most, but he smiled and rubbed his hands together. I think he enjoyed watching people suffer.

"C'mon, freak," Switzer growled, moving a crate to expose the small alien shaking behind a metal container.

"Stop it!" Ketheria yelled at him.

"Please, big thing. Please," Nugget begged as Switzer closed in. Switzer reached out for the alien, but Ketheria stepped in front of him. Even though Ketheria was eight years old now, she was still only half the size of Switzer.

"Stop," she said, holding up her hand.

"Get out of my way, freak," he said while taking a cautious step backward. Switzer never seemed comfortable around Ketheria after we found out about her mind-reading abilities.

I moved to intervene, but Theylor stepped between them.

"That will be enough, children," Theylor said. "Ketheria, could you bring Nugget to me, please?"

Ketheria knelt in front of Nugget and spoke softly to him. I could not hear what she was saying, but I knew he couldn't understand her anyway. She tickled him under the chin some more and then stood up, taking his big hand. Ketheria led Nugget over to Theylor and the R5.

"Thank you," Theylor said.

"Freak," Switzer mumbled under his breath.

"Nugget will not be hurt. As you all remember, the procedure is painless and only takes a moment to perform," Theylor said.

Theylor reached for Nugget's hand, but he wasn't having any of that, so Ketheria had to lead him over to the chairlike robot. She helped Nugget get comfortable and gently pressed his face down on the headrest.

"Please," Nugget whimpered.

"It's all right, Nugget," she comforted him and caressed his dark-purplish wings.

The robot shifted, making adjustments for Nugget's size. Nugget struggled to free himself, but the machine held him in place.

"Danger! Danger! Daaaaann . . . !"

Before Nugget could finish shouting, the R5 had implanted a small port at the back of Nugget's left ear.

"What about the codec?" I asked. The central computer interprets all of the different alien languages for us using a translation codec that is uplinked through the neural port. It even connects with your optical nerves so you can read in any language.

"This R5 is now equipped with the translation codec. Everything is done at once," Theylor said. "Nugget should now be able to understand everyone."

The R5 released Nugget, and he scrambled to the other side of the sorting bay.

"Danger! Danger! Danger!" he screamed, and found a crate to hide behind.

"Hey! Freak! Can you understand what I'm saying to you?" Switzer shouted at Nugget.

Nugget cocked his head to the side and slipped out from behind the crate.

"Yes?" Nugget said, but it was more like a question. He squinted his eyes and waited for a reply from Switzer. "Good. Now get out of here and leave us alone." Switzer pointed to Weegin's office. That was not a good idea. Nugget puffed out his chest and stomped his oversize feet toward Switzer.

"No. Work. Work! To work now, big thing!" Nugget cried, pointing at the conveyor belts and snapping his jaw.

"Work!"

"Great," Theodore said.

"Thanks, Theylor," I said. "I guess."

Nugget darted around the room corralling the other children and goading them toward the belts. Theylor smiled with his right head while his left head turned toward me. "Will you give this to your Guarantor please, Johnny?"

"Sure, Theylor," I said. "What is it?"

"You will know everything shortly," Theylor responded. I hated it when he was so vague. It usually meant something was about to change.

"And Johnny?" Theylor turned before he was out the door. "Enjoy Birth Day," said both of Theylor's heads, and then he was gone.

"It's Birth Day?" Theodore asked.

"I guess it is. Happy fourteenth," I said, just as surprised as the rest.

"What's on the scroll?" Max asked me, motioning to the glowing screen scroll the Keeper left for Weegin.

Max and Theodore stood there staring at me.

"How would I know?" I asked them.

"Take a peek." Max nudged me.

"Maybe he shouldn't do that," Theodore argued.

"Oh, give me that," Max said. She grabbed the scroll and unraveled the organic screen from its metal container. She pulled the uplink from the scroll and inserted it into her neural implant. The glow from the metal casing flashed: INVALID USER.

"Told you," Theodore said.

"Here, you do it," Max said, holding it out to me. "Do the *push* thing," Max said. She knew very well I could sneak into hard drives, network arrays, light drives, anything to do with a computer.

I was about to push into the scroll when an alarm went off. I looked up and saw the field portals at the top of the outer metal dome sparkle to life and begin to fade away. *Could a cargo shipment really be arriving?* I wondered. Nothing had come through those portals in over a phase. I stood next to Theodore and watched as the robotic cranes warmed up by stretching out their huge tentacles. But before they were in position, a small metal crate was thrust through the opening. It dropped from the sky like a meteor, right toward my sister.

"Ketheria, watch out!" I yelled and leaped forward, catching my sister's arm and yanking her aside.

"You all right?" Max questioned her.

Before she could answer, Weegin burst from his office and scurried down onto the sorting-bay floor.

"This has to be it. It has to be," he said, rubbing his three-fingered hands together.

"What *has* to be it?" Switzer said, inspecting the metal projectile.

"Shut up. Get back, you imbecile. Move away from here," Weegin scolded him.

Switzer simply stepped aside, scowling, but that didn't stop me from creeping forward. What was in the crate? I wondered.

"I said get out of here!" Weegin snapped before I could get close. "All of you. I'm deducting one chit for not listening." He used his small body to shield the contents of the crate. Nugget scrambled next to his father, but Weegin only pushed him aside.

"How can you deduct chits? You haven't paid us for a whole phase," Switzer protested.

Weegin ignored him and attached a thick data cable into his own neural port. He glanced over the ragged nubs on his shoulders to make sure none of us could see him tap an access code into the O-dat. Satisfied with Weegin's entry, the crate hissed open and Weegin jammed both fists inside the container. Quickly, he pulled out an unmarked plastic box and clutched it to his chest. His eyes darted over each of us without looking at anyone in particular. Then he grinned and raced off toward the lift. If Weegin still had wings, I'm sure he would have flown.

"I wonder what was inside," I said, walking over to the empty carcass Weegin had left behind.

"Nobody is to disturb me!" he shouted from the second floor as the latest messenger drone slammed into the closing office door.

"Never mind the crate, JT," Max said. "What does this scroll say?"

"Oh," I said, looking at the screen scroll still in my hands. I pushed into the scroll, and the message instantly appeared in my mind's eye as if an O-dat was mounted inside my forehead. I read it aloud.

Joca Krig Weegin,
As previously arranged by Keeper decree, the labor force of human beings is to be transferred to work duty on Orbis 2. Since all business for Joca Krig Weegin has been forfeited on every ring of Orbis, you are called upon to surrender your humans for immediate relocation.
CENTER FOR IMPARTIAL JUDGMENT AND FAIR DEALING

"Weegin has to give us back," I said, glancing up at his office.

"He's not going to like that. We're the only valuable thing he has right now," Max said.

"This is not good. I feel it," Ketheria muttered.

I looked over at Theodore, who was rummaging through the discarded shipping crate. He froze, his eyes widening. "And I think it just got worse," he added.

Get ready for all four adventures with JT and his friends on the Rings of Orbis.

PJ HAARSMA has always been transfixed by what lies beyond our solar system. He says, "When the mother ship finally arrives and they ask if there are any humans who want to go for a spin, I'll be the first to sign up." When he's not gazing at the stars waiting for his ride, PJ is the Executive Producer at Redbear Films where he created the hit show, Con Man with Alan Tudyk and Nathan Fillion. PJ is also the Co-Creator of Retro Replay and always trying to find new and interesting ways to bring his stories to life. He has a degree in science and lives in southern California with his wife and daughters. To learn more about PJ Haarsma, visit his website at www.pjhaarsma.com.

Made in the USA
Las Vegas, NV
09 December 2024